overboard

constellation edition

EM·SOLSTICE

Copyright © 2025 by Em Solstice

All rights reserved. No part of this publication may be reproduced, stored or transmitted in any form or by any means, electronic, mechanical, photocopying, recording, scanning, or otherwise without written permission from the publisher. It is illegal to copy this book, post it to a website, or distribute it by any other means without permission.

This novel is entirely a work of fiction. The names, characters and incidents portrayed in it are the work of the author's imagination. Any resemblance to actual persons, living or dead, events or localities is entirely coincidental.

First edition

ISBN 9798308338123

For T Cake,

Cause why choose right?

For Al,

Here's to all the books we've read

and all the fucks we've said

chapter one

TEN WEEKS IN ITALY is every girl's dream, except I wasn't here to sun it up on the beaches. Aunt Marie had managed to help me bag a job aboard Poseidon, a super yacht that chartered the coasts of the Mediterranean. I pushed my sunglasses above my head, brushing my hair back from my face. The size of the boat in front of me was unbelievable, the 54-metre boat was pristine white.

"I'm going to get lost." I mumbled to myself, slipping my sandals off on the hot deck floor to step onto the passerelle. Aunt Marie had taught me everything about yachting, mom and I had visited her on various boats during her free time while I was growing up.

I stepped onto the boat and followed the path down the side until I reached a door. I struggled to open the door and pull my suitcase through the narrow frame.

"Here let me get that for you." I jumped at the sound of another voice. The person offering to help me was over six feet tall, with curly brown hair, dark eyes and a bright smile. He was dressed in a teal t-shirt with a cursive 'P' and black shorts.

"Thank you." I smiled as he took my suitcase for me.

"I'm Phoenix, Bosun, and you must be Presley, our new stew?"

"That's me." I held out my hand to shake his. He wrapped his hand around mine lightly and then let go.

"Welcome aboard, so if you head through that door, up the stairs it will take you up to Cap. I'll take this down for you."

"Thank you so much." I placed my hand on my heart.

"Don't worry about it. I'd get going before Eve traps you before you've even seen the boat." I knew that Eve was the Chief Stew on the yacht and the person that would make my life easier or make it hell.

I followed Phoenix's instructions up to the bridge. The boat's interior was dark and had heaps of natural wood built into the interior. The control panel was black with oak accents. There was a small seating area at the back of the room with a table. Someone was sitting in the leather Captain's chair. The chair spun around and for a split second, I lost my breath. I expected someone older, compared to the old captains who had given me sweets when I was younger. The captain couldn't have been older than thirty-five. He had dirty blonde hair tucked behind his ears and stormy blue eyes, that made him the perfect vision of a Disney prince with four golden stripes on his epaulettes. It was like Poseidon himself was standing in front of me. The way his shirt was tight against the muscles underneath almost had me feeling faint. I'd never seen a hotter captain in my life.

"Hi, I'm- Presley." I stepped forward, hands behind me, pinching my skin to calm my nerves. The captain stood.

"Pleasure to have you on board, Presley. I'm Captain Xavier." He held out his hand for me to shake. I shook his hand with a small smile. "You came highly recommended by a mentor of mine. You're related to Marie Ramsey?" I nodded. I'd forgotten how people fought tooth and nail to have my aunt as Chief Stew.

"My aunt, she's been in the industry for about twenty years now, I think. Thank you for the opportunity, I know I don't have any professional yacht experience."

"I've read your resume, your skills will translate I'm sure." I nodded, and as I opened my mouth to speak, but another voice joined the bridge, coming from the doorway.

The woman was tall with beautiful blonde hair with matching thick brows. Her face had pointed features that belonged on the runway of a Victoria's Secret show.

"Xavier-" She started then spotted me. "Oh, hi." She forced a smile at me. The dreaded feeling hit me that I hadn't been paired with a nicey nice Chief Stew.

"Eve this is your new Stew." He put his hand on my shoulder. My entire body shivered. "Be nice." He warned her, which didn't help my nerves in the slightest.

"I always am." She plastered on a fake smile like a mean girl at school.

"Come on sweetie, let's get you your uniform and settled in." She strolled over to me, brushed Captain Xavier's hand off my shoulder and took my hand. As she tugged me off the bridge, her eyes lingered on the hot Captain and I didn't blame her.

chapter two

MY FIRST TWENTY-FOUR HOURS onboard already had me exhausted, I'd gone from a lazy Postgraduate student to running up and down flights of stairs. I'd hit my daily step goal halfway through the day and I hadn't managed to do that since last summer. Eve ran a strict interior, she wanted everything polished and rearranged before the first charter.

Our first charter wasn't new money looking for a good time and people to dance to their every whim, it was the owner of the yacht and a few of his friends. My nerves were already sky high without the added pressure. I was struggling to attach my epaulettes as Jameson, the Chef walked past.

"Hey, can you help me please?" I called out. The silver-haired Chef spun on his heel and stepped into my cabin.

"It's tricky isn't it?" He smiled at me. I think Jameson won my heart after he served the crew chilli last night. He was classically handsome, and naturally grey even though he was young.

"I've been fighting with them for five minutes and I'm worried Eve is going to kill me before my first charter." I chewed on my lip.

"You are going to do just fine, girlie." He straightened my collar. "Just keep your head down and do the best you can. You're green, no one expects you to be the perfect Stewardess and if you need any help, my galley is always open."

"Thanks, Jameson."

"We've all been on Poseidon together for a few years, it's hard being the new girl. But to let you into a little secret, there's a great year-round retainer." He whispered. I laughed a little as the radio called us to the dock to greet our guests.

"Sunnies!" I heard the shouting of my cabin mate. May dipped past James and me in the small space and snatched her sunglasses off her bed. May was the Lead Deckhand and the only girl on the Deck Team. She snored and listened to heavy rock way too loudly in her headphones, that even I could hear. I spent most of the night worrying that her eardrums were going to pop. "Come on, sweetie. This is an exciting charter." May grabbed my hand.

"Umm okay," I replied, looking over my shoulder to wave at Jameson.

May dragged me off the yacht to stand in line with the rest of the crew. I took my spot next to Chessa, the Second Stew. Jameson soon followed us out and stood next to Captain Xavier. At the end of the dock, I could see a group of people chatting amongst themselves.

The guy upfront slipped the shades off his eyes and hung them on the tight-fitting white shirt and pair of dark shorts. The closer he got the more I was in awe. Not only was my Captain hot, but so was my first charter guest, and I had to act completely professionally. My best friend Alicia had told me that Italy was full of hot men, but I didn't need two straight off the bat and two people that I could absolutely not go near.

"Hot isn't he?" May whispered. Now that the guest was closer I had a better look at him. His skin was a pristine gold, part of me was disappointed he wasn't covered in tattoos like the Captain, but the way he carried himself screamed powerful and fucking rich. "He's the owner." That was the second my heart stopped beating.

First charter. Hot guest. The owner.

My stomach churned and for a moment I wanted to catch the next flight back to the UK.

"His name is Killian." May whispered to me as he was steps away from us.

"Shh." Chessa scolded us, and I bit down on my lip, giving May the side eye. Chessa had been all business with me while teaching me how to turn around rooms and instructing me on how to turn them down. Later on, I saw her hanging around with Eve. Jameson's comment that they had all been a team for years rang true. They were loyal to one another, but some were obviously friendlier than others.

"Xavi!" Killian cheered as he hugged our Captain like an old friend. The Captain used one arm to hug him. The sound of his speech was slightly slurred, showing he was living his best life, he probably always lived his best life when you rented out your millions worth yacht for hundreds of thousands for a few days.

The other guests consisted of three women who looked like they stepped out of a Vogue magazine. There was another couple of guys with him, meaning three men to couple up with three beautiful women, which meant he was off the cards anyway. Killian made his way down the line of his crew, greeting them all with friendly chit chat, asking how their lives were and if they had a good rest over the winter period. When he stood in front of Chessa a wave of Tom Ford aftershave hit my nose and not booze.

Then it was my turn. My boss stood directly in front of me, his eyes examining every inch of me, checking over my uniform to make sure it was neat. Then his eyes met mine, dark fern green eyes.

"And you must be my new Third Stew, Presley, right?"

"Yes, sir." My voice was calm and put together. My hands clenched behind my back, my nails digging into my palms.

"Welcome to the team. I liked your resume. I'm excited about cocktail hour." He winked at me and moved on to May, greeting her with a hug. My attention was taken away from Killian as his guests said hello to me and introduced themselves.

"I'm assuming none of you need a tour, but if you do I'm happy to take you around the boat. If not we can head straight up to the aft deck and get you all some drinks." Eve stepped forward and clapped her hands together.

"Drinks would be great thank you, Eve." Eve passed me. "Laundry please." I nodded and she took the lead of the group to guide them onto the boat.

I took myself out of the way and down to the laundry. The cramped area barely had room to turn in, with the ironing board taking up most of the room. The sound of the washing machines rattled in my ears and I was left to my own devices. I was a third stew. I was probably going to spend most of the summer in laundry, and turning down rooms. If I was lucky I would get a shot at service, depending on the clientele. Hospitality was something I had always sunk my teeth into, my ultimate downfall of being a people pleaser, had sent me to my doom.

I hummed to myself as I folded and rolled the towels for the guests. The laundry room was down in the crew mess and occasionally one of the crew members would pass me. Just as I finished folding and organising the laundry, so that it worked for me, Chessa walked down with a stack of white napkins.

"Eve wants to know if you know how to fold napkins. You know, something fancy." She placed the stack on the ironing board.

"Yeah, I know a few patterns."

"Great, get these done and then let Eve know."

"Yeah sure. Is there a theme for dinner? Anything in particular?"

"No just something impressive. If you're struggling I can come show you how to do it but just bare in mind I'm busy on service." Her words were a little bit backhanded like I wasn't as busy as her. Chessa turned on her heel, her honey-brown hair swaying behind her and she went back upstairs.

I picked up the napkins and sat myself at the crew mess table to concentrate. Origami had been something my Dad taught me and what I loved the most about it was being able to use that skill in hospitality. I folded and twisted each of the crisp white napkins into a rose, using two corners to create leaves on either side. Once I was done I used the steamer to set each one in place and set them on the ironing board for dinner service.

I headed upstairs, taking me into the galley where Jameson was busy dicing various vegetables for dinner.

"How's the life of being a slave?" Jameson asked.

"Not bad, but ask me again in a couple of charters." I said to him, leaning against the free counter. "What are you cooking?" I asked.

"Tonight they are having truffle caprese salad, salmone alla griglia, and lemon cheesecake for dessert. "

"Oh my god, that sounds divine."

"I'll save you some cheesecake." Jameson looked up from his chopping board and winked at me.

"I'd love that."

"What I'd love is my Third Stew working instead of chatting away with the Chef." I whipped my head around so quickly that I strained my neck.

"Sorry I was-"

"Don't be such a hard ass Eve. She was asking about how I run the kitchen."

"My interior, Jameson, stay out of it." She glared and crossed her arms. "Have you done the napkins?"

"Yeah, they're on the ironing board. I was just coming to find you to see if you needed anything else."

"Go on your break, hour and a half. Then back up here to set up the table for dinner. Think you can manage that?" She snarked. I nodded. I knew it was best to keep my mouth shut. Part of me hoped that her attitude would change towards me when I wasn't the new girl. Although the words out of Jameson's mouth gave me the idea that she was always like this.

"No problem." I smiled, standing up straight.

"She's on break now, so you can go." Jameson glanced at her sideways. Eve scoffed and walked away to the Stew area, starting to make cocktails. Part of me wanted to offer my help but I also didn't have 'mug' written on my head. James flipped his finger off at her back and mouthed 'bitch'. I sniggered to myself and turned my head towards the window.

We'd left the dock and anchored during my time in the laundry. It was my first moment to take in the Italian scenery that would be my home for the next ten weeks. The sun reflected off the small swells of waves like the sea had been dipped in glitter.

I spent some of my free time talking to Jameson, then left him to cook. I sat in the corner of the crew mess booth and propped my phone up on a water bottle, calling Aunt Marie. I wasn't sure whether she would answer or not. Her charter yacht was in the South of France this summer, Chief Stew to a team of six stewardesses. When she answered my call, all I could see was the top of her head.

"Hey doll. You okay?" She peeked her eyes into the camera.

"Yeah, can you talk?"

"I'm just doing provisions, so I have a few minutes. How are you settling in?"

"I'm tired, but I'm sure it's just growing pains. I did the napkins for dinner, want to see?"

"Oh yes, show me!" I climbed over the booth, grabbed my phone and strolled over to the laundry area. I spun the camera around. "Here." Aunt Marie poked her head over.

"That's my girl. They're lovely. Has your Chief Stew seen them?" I turned the camera back, and shook my head. She examined my face. "Ah. I'm having a feeling."

"That I miss you? Yeah." I dragged out.

"Just take deep breaths, they're probably just stressed."

"Our first charter is the owner of the boat." I told her, sitting back down. "His name is Killian."

"Killian Westman?"

"Umm, no idea."

"He's in the clubbing industry. What's your boat called?"

"Poseidon."

"Yeah, that's him. I know a couple of people that have worked on his boat. He'll be a good start for you. Have you decided what you're planning to do after the season?" I shrugged.

"No idea, just concentrating on the next few weeks. Hopefully, I'll make enough to get me through a few months."

"I do wish you'd consider staying in yachting, you'd be a brilliant Chief with some experience." She sighed.

"I might, I don't know yet."

"Okay, doll. Right, I need to call my supplier, but text me before you go to bed?"

"Yeah sure." I laughed. "Love you, bye."

"Love you, doll." I hung up the call, just as Jameson walked downstairs, three large wrapped dishes stacked in his arms.

"Grubs up." He placed the dishes on the table, setting them out. "Chicken fajitas."

"You're my new favourite person." I told him, taking the foil off the top of the casserole dish. Jameson was good, the entire dish was like a rainbow, peppers, onions, and juicy flavoured chicken all mixed together.

"I was already aware, girlie. Enjoy. You got enough time to eat?" He asked. I nodded.

"Yeah, I still have twenty minutes."

"Okay, I need to go start cooking for Killian. See you later."

Mid-way through eating, Eve called on the radio for us to get into our blacks. After I finished eating I did as Eve asked, changing into my clothes. I called on the radio to see where I was needed to help set up for dinner service.

I carefully piled the napkins into a basket and carried them up to the aft deck to join Chessa in setting up. The doors opened automatically and I stepped onto the deck. Chessa was laying out the plates on the table.

"I have the napkins," I announced and she looked up.

"Do you know how to lay the table?" She asked.

"Yeah, I know how."

"I'll leave you to do this then and I'm going to collect glasses."

"Yeah, no problem."

"White gloves are on the side with the cutlery." Chessa disappeared.

I pulled on the white gloves and began setting out the shiny silver cutlery. I placed my napkins on the centre of the plates and straightened the flowers in the centre of the table. Chessa returned with a tray of wine glasses and handed them to me. Then went back for champagne glasses. I stood back once the table was finished and smiled. My rose napkins went perfectly with the decor that had been pulled. There was a mixture of blue and white flowers in the centre of the table with pearls snaked throughout, with silk tablecloth.

Eve stepped out onto the deck.

"Wow, Chess, this looks great." Eve gave her second a side hug.

"Thanks, hot stuff."

"So the guests are about to come up I think. Presley, you need to stock the mini fridge in the lounge and then once all the guests are up, you can do cabins."

"Sure." I smiled and headed back inside the boat. I checked the fridge behind the bar, making a mental note of the things I needed to get. Water. Cola. Lemonade. One thing I liked about yachting was how much quicker you could be on your feet when you had bare feet to run around on.

I was crouched behind the bar with the stacks of drinks that I was restocking. I could hear the guests chatting amongst themselves until Eve joined them.

"Are you all ready to be seated?" She asked. There was a chorus of agreement, and the patter of feet passed me. I glanced to my left to see their reaction to the table decor.

"Wow, Eve, who made those napkins, they are the cutest!" I heard Lily, one of the guests.

"That would be me. Do you like it?" My mouth could have dropped when the blatant lie dropped from her mouth. I was her Stew, but it didn't mean that what I did she got the credit for. The look on my face was murderous, and the person who was looking straight at me from my hiding spot shouldn't have seen it. Killian was looking straight at me. I hadn't seen him since he got on the boat this afternoon. I looked away and carried on stocking the fridge, chewing on my lip, getting a taste of my lip balm, and trying to remember what my Aunt had said about the fact Eve was probably stressed.

chapter three

"Presley, Presley, are you in the cabins?" Eve called through the radio.

"Working on the VIP cabin and about to start the master," I answered. There was no answer back, which rattled me even further. A thank you would have been nice at least. I took a deep breath and collected the rubbish bag from the floor.

I got rid of the rubbish and stopped by the crew mess to grab my phone and AirPods. As long as I still had my radio in my ear, I could work with one earphone in, surely. I needed something that would keep me rooted, which happened to be my love, Lewis Capaldi.

I started on the master cabin, straightening the sheets and turning back the corners. I cleaned up the few clothes that had been left on the floor, folding them neatly and putting them onto the chair. I turned off the main lights and turned on the various lamps around the room.

The shiny wooden effect from the rest of the boat, the fluffy cream carpet, and the super king-size bed that was going to be a bitch to change. Opposite the bed was a huge flat screen and a cabinet underneath, behind the wall was the master bathroom with a jacuzzi bathtub, his and hers sinks, toilet and shower, which were also separated by decorative frosted glass, golden quartz floors and a piece above the bath.

I wiped down the entire bathroom, so every surface sparkled under the spotlights. I dimmed the lights in the bathroom and reentered the master cabin to close the blinds.

"So, before you go. Was there something I could've said to make your heart beat better? If only I'd known you had a storm to weather." I sang to myself. When I turned on my heel I screamed. Shadowing the master cabin doorway, Killian was standing in a light blue dress shirt covered in red wine. My eyes blew and I snatched my AirPod from my ear and then stuffed it into my back pocket.

"Sir, I am so s-"

"Don't worry about it. If music helps you work, then it helps you work. Although I would be careful on charters."

"Of course. I just- It's my first- I'm nervous." I stumbled.

"I can tell. If it makes you feel better, Chessa just tripped over her own feet and spilt wine on me." He motioned to the deep red stain on his chest. The fabric sticking to his chest, right on his abs. I looked away quickly although looking at his green eyes wasn't much better.

"Would you like me to get the stain out for you?" I smiled.

"That would be great." I didn't expect him to start stripping off his shirt in front of me.

Killian was carved by gods, his abs were beyond defined. He was lean rather than bulky, and when his arms flexed taking off his shirt. I stepped forward and took it from him.

"No problem, I've had to get a few red wine stains out over the years." I joked.

"You like red wine?" He asked, pulling out a new black shirt, and then pulling it over his shoulders.

"Only when I'm drunk, which is why I end up with stains." I examined the red wine stain, it was pretty bad and I'd probably call my mom for some tips. There was no doubt that the shirt I was holding was a couple of hundred pounds at least.

"Are you enjoying yourself so far?" He buttoned up his shirt, stepping towards me until there were only a couple of centimetres between us. It meant I had to look up at him. Killian was towering over me like he had when he first came aboard.

"It's a nice change of pace. I just graduated a couple of months ago."

"Hospitality?" He asked.

"Yeah." I whispered. Killian made me feel small and not in a bad way like he was wrapping me up and keeping me safe. The proximity was making me sweat slightly, and I was afraid he was close enough to see sweat beads drip down my forehead. My heart was fast and loud in my ears.

"Is this where you want to be? Yachting? Tell me honestly."

"I don't know. It's in my blood. But right now I'm not sure what my dream is." Killian smiled at me, and his eyes met mine.

"Here's your challenge, by the end of the season I want you to be able to tell me." His eyes dropped to my lips for a split second then back to my eyes. We were almost touching, and if I were in any other situation I'd be closing that space. Though I hoped he was going to do it anyway.

"Why?" I tilted my head.

"I believe in my staff. I want them to be the best version of themselves, and to know who they are."

"Okay." I couldn't make promises, but even if I could give out some bullshit answers at the end of the season, if I was lucky maybe I could land myself a bonus. At that moment though I wanted to say anything that would please Killian.

"I'm going to head back upstairs to eat, but I hope to see you on service tomorrow." I held back my scoff, something gave me the feeling that Eve was more than happy keeping me down in the cabins and laundry. I didn't think I'd be able to use any of my bar skills over the next two months.

"Enjoy your meal, sir."

"Thank you and call me Killian."

"Enjoy your meal, Killian. And I will get your shirt sorted for you." Killian stepped back and I watched him leave the room. Once I heard the tap on his shoes fade away I took a deep breath, sweeping my hair back.

"You're a fucking idiot." I mumbled to myself. "You could have lost your job."

I wanted to kiss him. I wished that I had kissed him. I brought his shirt up to my nose like some sort of creepy gremlin, taking in the expensive smell of Tom Ford.

"Presley, Presley, Eve, after cabins go into laundry and knock off in an hour. Up at 6.30."

chapter four

I THOUGHT BEING THE 'early worm' would mean I would get a chance at breakfast service, but the second the guests had woken up, Chessa was there and I didn't get a chance to even say good morning. I was sent back down into the cabins and unlike last night I didn't get to see Killian. After I'd done the cabins and washed the crew uniform that had been dumped in the laundry cubby I walked into the galley to offer my services to Jameson to help clean up after breakfast.

"Hey do you need help?" I skipped into the galley.

"If you could wash those pans up, I owe you a drink when we get a night off." He waved his knife towards the sink where pans were piling up.

"I got you." I told him. I took off my watch and left it on the side before running the hot tap and adding soap to be able to wash up for him. "How did breakfast go?"

"Killian and his friends are a breeze. I like that he's always the first charter of the season and pops back throughout, it's calming. I know everything he likes ya know." He said flipping over some bacon.

"Yeah, it's nice." I agreed.

"How are you feeling?" Jameson asked, dishing the crispy bacon into a dish for us crew.

"I'm okay. I slept like a log and did not want to get up this morning. I was hoping to be on service. I haven't had a chance yet." I told him

"Eve can be a bit like that. Don't worry, if it carries on, I'll say something."

"You don't need to do that." I told him while starting to wash the pans.

"I told you I had your back and how are you ever meant to learn if you're not given a chance. You have experience right?"

"Yeah, I worked in a bar during Uni, and my parents own this cute little tourist restaurant on the Cornish coast."

"That sounds so peaceful, do they need a chef?" He joked.

"You're welcome anytime my darling." I gave him a big smile and Jameson blew me a kiss.

"I'm making bacon ice cream later, and you are getting some."

"Can't wait."

"Good morning." Captain Xavier walked into the kitchen, dressed in his casual blue polo and a pair of black shorts. His wild dark blonde hair was brushed back with a pair of sunglasses on his head. He walked over to the coffee machine and pushed in a coffee pod. "How was breakfast, James?" He asked, putting his cup in place and turning on the machine.

"Good, Cap. As always I haven't heard any complaints." I giggled at Jameson's cute ego.

"That's what I like to hear. A good start to the season, and I hope you're going to keep it up." I dried my hands on a towel and folded it back up on the side near the sink. Eyes were burning into the back of my head and I turned around to find the captain looking at me. I smiled politely and nodded at him. "How are you getting on Presley?"

"I'm settling in."

"Eve hasn't put her on service at all." Jameson butted in, my mouth dropped open and I looked at him in shock. Clearly he had no issue about speaking his mind.

"Any reason why?" Captain Xavier asked.

"You know what she is like Cap when it comes to new Stews. It's unfair and we all know it." Jameson slung his towel over his shoulder and stood against the counter with his arms folded. Captain Xavier picked up his coffee and took a scorching sip.

"Come with me, Presley." He ordered.

"Um, sure." I chewed on my lip and followed Captain Xavier out of the galley and towards the bridge. I was slightly nervous. The last thing I wanted to do was make an enemy of the woman who decided when I slept or not. My entire season would be fucked.

"Take a seat." Captain Xavier nodded to the seating area behind the controls. I perched myself on the edge and watched with anticipation as he picked up his phone and dialled a number. "Come up to the bridge…yeah, see you in a second." He chucked his phone onto the chair and took a seat next to me.

I was thrown into another situation where I was in close proximity to a man who made my heart beat faster. The seating area was fairly decent but the Captain was broad and took up a large amount of space. Our knees were almost touching and I couldn't do anything but squeeze mine closer together, so they wouldn't touch.

The door leading outside swung open and my breath hitched at the sight of Killian who was in nothing but his swim shorts, drying his hair with a towel, and water beads dripping down his chest. Killian's eyes met mine and his brows furrowed.

"What's going on?" He sounded annoyed and my heart beat faster in my chest. I was screaming at Jameson inside of my head for getting involved.

"She isn't in trouble. We're just having a few...growing pains again, with Eve." Captain Xavier spoke. Killian sighed and glared at Xavier, although anyone could tell it was Eve that he was really pissed with. A part of me was glad that I wasn't the only person she had given the dirty work to.

Killian turned to me and his fern-green eyes softened as he smiled at me. He leaned on his shoulder against the wall beside me.

"What's happened, love?" Love. I should have been speaking to HR about my boss and inappropriate nicknames but my heart was floating around my chest like a butterfly. I was wedged between them both at this point, my skin was on fire and they hadn't even touched me, although the whorish part of me was considering asking. I went to speak twice trying to force myself to speak.

"Exactly what happened last year. Eve is keeping her third completely cut off from service and down in the cabins." Captain Xavier spoke for me.

"I see." There was a moment between Xavier and Killian that I couldn't quite figure out, one look was like a whole conversation between them. "I'll talk to her. I was going to request a cocktail hour after dinner. I'll tell her that I want you there." Killian told me.

"Thank you. I don't want to cause Eve any trouble though it's only been a couple of days, I'm sure she's just trying to figure out my skill set."

"Eve knows your skill set and we know what she can be like. My Chief Stew is good at her job, but sometimes she gets in over her head. Besides, I would love to see more of you before I go."

Holy shit. This man was trying to get me sectioned before my first week was even over. There was no hiding that my cheeks were flushed red, I dipped my head hoping that my bangs would cover my cheeks. I began picking at my skin with my nails. Xavier's hand crossed mine pulling my hand away.

Inappropriate was beyond the word that I needed to describe the skin on skin contact with my Captain while my boss stood over us. I locked eyes with Xavier and pulled my hand away despite what I actually wanted to do, which was interlink our fingers, and compare how tiny my hands were to his. I looked at Killian afraid that I was going to be punished, or if Xavier was going to be punished. Except he was the vision of calm.

"Why don't you go check on my shirt for me, love? I need to have a chat with Xavi."

"Umm, yeah. Sure. I'll just go do that." I spewed and jumped up from my seat ready to flee the scene, as I brushed past Killian he grabbed my hand.

"You best make me something special later." He raised a brow.

"Of course sir." He let go of me and I rushed out of the bridge, leaving the men to talk.

I found myself a quiet corner of the ship, stowed away in a corner where I could take a moment to take some deep breaths and put myself back together. I hadn't wanted to pull away my hand from either of them. I almost felt at peace and safe, but I also forgot that I had a job to do and I needed the money. Not to be screwing around with my bosses and landing myself in a situation that would send me back home with my tail between my legs.

"Pres?" Elliot, the deck hand, found me. I smiled.

"Sorry I was just taking a second. A little overwhelmed with everything going on. Please don't tell Eve."

"Tell the dragon?" He scoffed. "Not a chance. But if you need somewhere to hide, the deck crew can always hide you away with the toys." He winked and walked away.

I gave myself another second before getting myself back to work, and my first job was in the galley. I navigated myself back without getting lost and crept up behind Jameson, then I whacked him around the head. He jumped up from writing his menu and spun to face me.

"Ow, what was that for?"

"You didn't need to tell Captain Xavier. I was fine."

"Oh please, you would have been stuck cleaning for weeks before he even noticed. I was just speeding up the process. Did it work?"

"Did what work?" May strolled in and picked an apple up from the fruit bowl.

"I told Cap that Eve has Pres stuck on boring ass duties and not giving her a chance on service."

"Oh good idea." She mumbled, her mouth full of her apple. I rolled my eyes.

"Guys." I warned.

"We have your back. It's what you wanted right?" Jameson put his arm around my shoulder. I nodded.

"It would be nice." And I'd get to spend time with Killian. Not alone. Not like a part of me wanted but at least I would be in his dominating presence.

"Then just go with the flow." May nudged me. "Cap and Killian will tell her it's their idea anyway. They know how to handle her."

"Okay, okay, thank you." I leaned into Jameson. I was beyond lucky that I had already made two good friends aboard the boat because without them I think the homesickness would have really kicked in. "I need to go check on Killian's shirt that he spilled red wine on. So I'll see you guys later."

Luckily the wine stain had come out from the soft baby blue fabric. I hung it up on a hanger and scrawled out a note to attach to it. 'Told you I could get it out, let me know if you want it pressed. Presley.' I returned the shirt to his room and went to find either of the other stews to see if there was anything I could help with.

Chessa was bringing in table decor from breakfast, and Eve was serving Marshall and Zoey at the bar.

"I can take those if you want?" I held out my hands. Chessa passed the decor over.

"Thanks." She brushed past me.

"No problem," I mumbled and walked to the hallway to put the decor away. As I juggled with the different decor, trying to put it back correctly Eve snuck up behind me and nearly scared the life out of me.

"You're going to have to have a three hour break just before we start dinner service. Killian requested you to be their bartender tonight." Eve did not look happy with me, as much as she tried to hide it.

"Yeah, okay. I can do that." While I tried to hide the fact I was beyond happy to be doing something worthwhile.

"After you've cleared the decor. The boat needs hoovering. Top to bottom. Can you handle it?"

"Yes, I'm pretty sure I can hoover." I fought the urge to roll my eyes at her. Everyone was right Eve loved to treat her Third Stew as some sort of idiot.

"Good." Eve turned back around and headed back to her post at the bar to fill up the guests' empty glasses.

I smiled to myself, and my heart skipped a beat at the thought of being able to spend the night around Killian, even if I was working.

chapter five

I SCREAMED NEARLY FALLING out of my bunk as my alarm woke me up. Underneath me I heard the giggling of May.

"Oh shush." I laughed.

"That was the highest scream I've ever heard, you nearly burst my eardrum."

"I nearly broke my coccyx, bitch." I jumped down from the top bunk and stretched out my body in the tiny space of our cabin.

"By the end of the season, I guarantee you will have fallen out of that bunk."

"I mean all of this space on the boat and the crew get the finest cabins. Do guests really need those extra couple of square metres?" I sighed while switching on the light. May groaned. "Are you off or on break?" I asked.

"Off, but I had a red bull an hour ago so I have a few more hours until I fall asleep." She shrugged, scrolling through her phone. I threw on my black skirt. I slipped on the skirt and added the belt then tamed my hair back in a low ponytail. Luckily I only needed a little bit of face powder to tidy up where my face had leant on the pillow and added a fresh layer of mascara.

"Okay well, I am off to serve cocktails to a bunch of people already stupidly drunk." I said throwing on my black shirt and buttoning it up.

"Killian being drunk is like being around one of the nicest people in the world. He likes to just hand out cash."

"He seems way too generous to be a successful businessman." I said opening the door.

"Eh, the guy owns a yacht but he isn't very materialistic." May said.

"See you in the morning." I smiled

"Night, girlie." I shut the cabin door and jogged up the stairs into the galley. I was met by a mean looking blonde bitch also known as my Chief Stew.

"You're two minutes late. When you're late you're knocking into other people's sleep. It's not on."

"Oi, Eve. Remember that time you were two hours late while you were showing your boyfriend your tits on FaceTime and Chessa barely got any sleep?" Jameson popped his head out of the galley, while biting into an apple. Eve glared at him, but she didn't dare say anything else. Chefs pulled rank over a Chief Stew on a yacht and having Jameson on my side was proving to be a good thing. Eve didn't dare argue with him over anything, unless it was about service and she knew she hadn't a leg to stand on.

"It won't happen again." I told her with a smile. Keep your friends close and your enemies closer. I didn't want to give Eve any ammunition against me no matter how of a bitch she was to me.

"Make sure it doesn't." Eve brushed past me. "The guests are in the main salon."

"Okay, thank you." I called, then turned to Jameson. "Is it just me up?"

"You and Elliot, he's on deck. I'm going to head to bed, are you going to be okay?"

"Runs in my blood."

"Yeah, what I wouldn't do to swap Eve for your Aunt Marie." He dumped his apple core in the bin and kissed the top of my head. "Night Pres."

"Night James." James walked down into the crew mess and I made my way to the main salon where the guests were all gathered around the sofa area. I took a deep breath before I announced myself.

"Evening everyone, what can I get everyone?" I pulled a big smile onto my face. My eyes locked with Killian's and his mouth turned up into a subtle smile.

"Let's break you in shall we, Presley?" Chris sat forward. Chris was conventionally handsome, he had soft features and a head of black hair, which made him look like a smouldering model for GQ magazine.

"How about you surprise us for the first round?" Killian spoke up.

"That I can do. Fruity?" There was a chorus of yes and I walked towards the bar. I kneeled down and looked in the fridge for what we had in there. There were some fresh strawberries and raspberries, so I pulled those out and placed them on the bar. I grabbed six martini glasses and the cocktail set.

I muddled the berries into a puree and added cranberry juice, vanilla vodka, strawberry liqueur and lemon juice, topped with ice. Killian excused himself from his friends and came over to the bar. I inhaled a deep breath and hoped that I wasn't going to make a fool of myself. I knocked a glass into the shaker and began mixing it together. Killian's eyes were burning into me as I threw the shaker around, I was prepared for it to go everywhere and carried on breathing when it didn't. I pulled off the glass on top and grabbed the strainer. The first one only filled two glasses, so I repeated the same recipe twice more until each glass was filled. As I prepared to take the glasses over on a tray, Killian's hand caught my wrist.

"Don't worry, they can grab their own drinks." He told me. Killian called over his guests and they all crowded around the small bar area, each taking a glass.

"Wow, that is good." Zoey told me as she looked at Killian. "Keep this one, Kills." She lifted her glass as other compliments were directed at me. My cheeks flushed red and I looked down at the bar as they returned to their seats.

Two fingers lifted my chin, my breath hitched when I met his eyes. I quickly glanced over at the other guests, hoping they weren't watching the exchange. But how much would they care, Killian was the owner and could do whatever he wanted. I'd let him do whatever he wanted. How could I say no to my boss?

"Be proud of yourself." He whispered. "You deserve the praise, and I expect you'll get a lot of it in the next two months." His knuckles brushed along the edge of my jaw and then he rested his thumb on my cheek for a split second before dropping his hand and raising his glass.

I watched him walk away from me, my lips slightly parted as he sat back down on the sofa, his arm resting around the back of the sofa, around Lily and my heart clenched for a moment. It was jealousy, jealousy for a man I barely knew but had captured my complete attention.

I made sure the drinks were flowing, martinis weren't big and they didn't take long to drink. So to ensure that the guests weren't waiting long for drinks I prepped the puree while they were drinking, so it wouldn't take as long. I was impressed with how well I handled myself. Elliot popped into the salon and took glasses down to be washed then brought them back which was a big help to me. Killian didn't come back over to me, but there were glances at any moment he could before he was wrapped back into another conversation with his friends. Despite his arm being near Lily, they never got closer to one another and I was glad I didn't have to watch him get off with someone, who was actually lovely, and I didn't want to end up hating.

After a few hours, the guests started to go to bed and it gave me more time to make sure things were tidy for when Chessa and Eve woke up. It ended up with it being just Chris and Killian awake, they turned to whiskey a couple of hours ago. Killian had only had one glass that entire time, nursing it like it was the last glass of whiskey in existence. Chris downed the last few drops in his glass and stood.

"I'm heading to bed, mate." He looked over at me. "Thanks for the cocktails tonight, Presley."

"I was more than happy to serve them for you guys. I'm so glad you enjoyed them." I replied. Kilian stood and gave his friend one of those typical manly hugs.

It was just Killian and me, well Elliot was still out on deck. I swallowed as he walked towards the bar and placed his empty glass on the counter.

"I'll take another whiskey please, love. On the sun deck."

"Of course, sir."

"I told you to call me Killian." He raised an eyebrow.

"Sorry, Killian. I'll bring your whiskey up." Killian nodded and walked out onto the deck.

I prepared a fresh glass with ice and poured another glass of Whiskey for him. Elliot walked in, yawning.

"Killian just ordered me to bed." Elliot spoke. "I'll stay up if you need me to."

"No it's okay. It's only him and I'm sure he won't be up much longer." Elliot nodded.

"Night Presley."

"Night Elliot."

I picked up Killian's glass and walked out, heading up to the sun deck where Killian was waiting for me, no not me, his whiskey.

chapter six

THE BREEZE WAS BLOWING lightly as I walked up to the sun deck. Killian was lounging on one of the chairs near the hot tub, looking out to the sea. The small swells were reflecting the moonlight, it was undeniably stunning. I plastered a smile on my face, hoping to hide how nervous I was feeling as I passed the glass over to him. Our fingers touched and I bit down on my lip.

"Is there anything else I can get you?" I asked.

"Sit with me." He nodded to the chair beside him.

"I'm on shift, I can't. I'm just here to make your drinks and make sure you have everything that you need." I attempted to get out of it. He raised his brow at me and tilted his head.

"Sit." He ordered. The tone of his voice had changed. I imagined it to be the same voice he used in a business meeting, the tone would turn a grown man to putty in his hands. That's what I felt at that moment.

I perched myself on the edge of the seat, ready to jump up in case anyone came up to the sun deck. Someone had to be on anchor watch, but they wouldn't be able to leave their post anyway.

"Have you thought about what I asked you last night?"

"I haven't had much time to think, I've been working."

"Don't forget, okay? I want to know your dream in eight weeks' time." He took a sip of his whiskey.

Killian sat back in his seat, legs open, slouched in his position, his shirt had risen slightly and I got the chance to see a glimpse of his abs again. My eyes were attached and I wasn't as smooth as I thought.

"Enjoying yourself, love?" Every time he called me love my heart skipped a beat and my brain stopped working for a moment. I tried to answer but nothing would come out of my mouth. My cheeks were burning red. "Don't be embarrassed, I've just been a little bit more subtle when I've been watching you." He was crossing a line, no boss should say that to an employee, but I didn't care and I was stone cold sober.

"What exactly have you been watching?" I asked, forcing myself to be confident.

"If I tell you, am I going to end up in an HR complaint?" He chuckled. I shook my head.

"I wouldn't do that."

"And why is that?" He sat up, placing his glass on the small table between the chairs then leaning on his knees.

"For the same reason I've been watching you." I answered. Because Killian was crafted by gods.

"I've been watching the way your ass moves in that pretty skirt and wishing I'd ordered them a couple of inches shorter." I don't think there was any possible way of stopping my eyes blowing up like a cartoon character. "Come here." He jerked his head.

Moving on autopilot and not using my brain, I stood and stepped in front of him. He opened his legs wider and tugged me closer in between them by my thighs. I stumbled and had to catch myself using his shoulders to hold me up. His hands trailed up the back of my thighs, touching the hem of my skirt. He folded up the hem so that my skirt rested on the curve of my ass. The bottom of my cheeks would be on display if I walked.

"Just like this." He whispered, looking up at me. "Now if you were just my sole Stew, if it was just you and I on this boat then I'd make a few more alterations."

"Like?" My voice cracked and my heart was beating so fast in my ears, that I could barely hear myself.

"Presley. I don't want to take advantage of you. So don't test me if you don't want this." I didn't know what 'this' meant but I had an idea. A part of me felt like I was taking advantage of him, considering I'd been pouring him alcohol for hours.

"Like?" I repeated myself. There was no turning back.

Killian grabbed my thighs again and pulled me onto his lap so that I was straddling him. The cold air hit my ass. There wasn't a lot of stretch in our skirts, the fabric had completely rolled up to my hips. My lace red bikini briefs on show. My arms were wrapped around the back of his neck.

Killian's face was in the perfect position for a view of my boobs. He reached up in the small gap and managed to undo my shirt button. His eyes locked onto mine the entire time. Then he undid the next, and again, until four buttons were undone and he had a view of my cleavage.

"Your pretty tits would be on show too. The deck team would try and get glimpses of your ass and tits but I'd have you too busy running around after me that they wouldn't get a chance." He whispered to me. I could hear my short but heavy breaths as he spoke to me. "I'd make you wear your white shirt so I could see this pretty matching red set through it, while serving the Captain and I dinner." I squeezed my eyes shut, mentioning Captain Xavier burst the floodgates. The heat between my legs was pulsing, I could feel the wetness touching the lace and I tried to hold myself up so he wouldn't feel it on his jeans.

"My perfect little stewardess at my beck and call." He unbuttoned another. "Doing as she's told. A people pleaser." Another. "How far would you go to do a good job for me?" I wanted to answer but I was too concentrated on the feeling of my shirt being completely undone. I was almost bare in front of him. It wasn't like my clothes were doing anything, my shirt open and my skirt rolled up at my hips.

"Look at me." He ordered. I opened my eyes and looked down. "I know you're hovering on me, love. Sit." I gulped and relaxed on his lap, the damp fabric touching his jeans. Killian grabbed my ass and pulled me in closer, my pussy sitting on top of his straining cock. He was hard, I guessed painfully so.

"Are you like this with all your Stews?" I tilted my head. Maybe that's why Eve hated me. A hard smack came down on the top of my ass cheek and I squealed.

"No. Just you. Those pretty doe eyes had me from the moment I was sent your resume." I nodded in reply. "Little miss perfect and I knew I wanted to ruin you. Ruin you for any other man you'd meet on this boat. Because I own you now, Presley."

"Someone could come up at any time." I whispered.

"I just told you I want you to walk around half naked on this boat and you think someone coming up would bother me? Stop me?" His hand reached up and pulled the hair tie, freeing my hair. It fell around my face and I knew I would have clear tie kinks in it which annoyed me.

"I don't want to lose my job."

"Your job is safe. Xavier and I are the only people that could fire you, trust me when I tell you that isn't going to happen." Killian looked up, his eyes trained to my lips. It was like a ticking time bomb waiting for him to make the first move. He was teasing me, even with how hard he was beneath me.

I took the dive, I leant down, smashed his lips into mine. His lips tasted like smoked whiskey and berries. His hands gripped my ass and my body naturally grinding against him, rubbing my damp lace over his jeans. The friction sent sparks to my clit. I whimpered into the kiss because it just wasn't enough, I tried to grind harder wanting to feel the outline of his cock up and down my pussy.

Killian pulled away from me, we were both out of breath and my cheeks were burning. I couldn't read the look on his face and I was worried I had made a fool of myself, that he didn't want me as much as he said he did. A man with that much money could afford to play games with lowly stewardesses.

"Stand for me." He ordered softly. I complied and stood from his lap, missing the warmth from his hard on. I looked down at myself, I was an utter mess, and a whore, there was no denying it. "Take off your shirt and skirt." I let my black shirt drop to the floor, undid my belt to loosen my skirt then let it join my shirt. I stepped out of my skirt and stood in front of Killian in a matching red lace set. It must have been hard to see under the dim lighting on the sky deck.

Killian stood up and walked over to the day bed that covered the width of the deck. He unbuttoned his shirt and threw it to the side, then moved onto his jeans. He looked over his shoulder at me watching him, tugging off his jeans.

"Crawl to me." He called quietly, as he took a seat on the day bed, his knees up and resting his arms there. Even under the dim lighting I could see the strain in his boxers. His thick length also popped from the waistband. I swallowed and went down onto my hands and knees. My eyes trained on Killian as he licked his lips.

My tits were almost falling out of my bra as I slowly crawled towards him. The ache between my own legs had me stumbling, we'd only kissed and my whole body was begging for him. I looked over my shoulder at the stairs behind me.

"Eyes on me, love." I turned back to Killian, who had taken his cock from his boxers and had his hand wrapped around himself, slowly fucking himself with his hand. He was thick, a decent length, but the thickness of him was bound to tear me apart.

I reached his place on the day bed, watching him swipe his finger over the leaking head of his cock. He reached forward, forcing his thumb into my mouth. I tasted the precum on his thumb, less salty than I expected. I hallowed my cheeks out on his thumb and pretended it was the thick cock that he had in his hand. He pulled his thumb away and grabbed me by the cheeks.

"As much as I want that pretty mouth wrapped around my cock and gagging, there's another hole that's begging to be filled before I leave tomorrow."

"Please." I whispered.

"Again." He smirked.

"Please. Please fuck me."

"Are you on contraception?" I nodded frantically, the thought of using a condom made me almost sad. I needed to feel him inside of me with no barrier, and quickly. "Take off your underwear." I sat up on my knees and tugged down the red lace quickly, sitting on my ass to kick them on then returned to my knees. Killian squeezed his dick and moaned, staring at my bare pussy. "Here now." He ordered, taking off his boxers completely, his cock slapped against his abs. "Stand." I stood.

"Yes sir." I smirked and carefully walked towards him, keeping my balance on the soft furnishings. He tugged me closer as soon as he could.

My pussy was directly in front of his face. Killian dragged a finger down, then suddenly applied enough pressure that his finger slipped right into my pussy. I gasped as he curled his finger inside of me.

"No, I can't wait any longer." Before I could ask him what he meant, his face was buried between my legs. I wrapped my fingers into his hair trying to steady myself and not scream loud enough to wake the whole boat.

His lips were latched around my clit, sucking, and biting lightly, causing more wetness between my legs. His mouth moved lower, his tongue finding my hole that was begging to be filled with him. He moaned against my pussy, lapping up every drop between my legs like a man starved. My legs were trembling, trying to find the strength to keep me up. Little moans escaped my mouth, which was all I would allow myself.

The knot in my stomach was churning and growing as he slipped two fingers into my pussy and his mouth returned to my clit. His fingers went quicker and harder. The wetness of my pussy could be heard over the sound of the soft waves.

"Fuck." I mumbled. "Stop please, Killian. Stop before-" There was no way he was going to stop because Killian had been right where he wanted me, and that was being ruined by him. A moan which I had been holding back escaped my mouth as the knot in my stomach unravelled and I came on Killian's face.

My legs gave way from underneath me, but Killian caught me and lowered me down onto the bed. He hovered over me, hand on either side of my head, he pushed himself down capturing my mouth in a heavy kiss that I could taste myself in. I tried to stop him pulling away, lifting my head to keep my lips on his but he moved back too far.

"Lift your knees." He whispered. I lifted my knees up and Killian settled in between them, he grabbed my hips, tilting them up and he slipped inside of me without much pressure despite the size. My first orgasm had relaxed my body to become a perfect fit for him. My eyes almost rolled into the back of my head as he slowly pushed as deep as he possibly could, hitting my cervix and making me wince. It felt good having him that deep inside of me, and I realised how disappointing my sex life was that every other man I had been with couldn't do that. Killian had been right about ruining me for every other man. I had no doubts about him following through with his threat.

His pace started to quicken, I wrapped my arms around the back of his neck and wrapped them in the hair at the nape of his neck. I pulled him down to kiss me as he pumped his throbbing cock inside of me. His pace turned up a notch again. His heavy balls slapping against me. It still wasn't quick enough, or deep enough. I found myself needing the next level like a greedy slut. He broke our kiss and I watched his eyes fill with pure lust as he went deep inside of me.

"Fuck, love." He mumbled. I was already sensitive from my first orgasm that the next one was swelling inside of me quickly.

"Killian." I whimpered, squeezing my eyes shut and holding myself back so I didn't cause it to end too quickly.

"You're so fucking tight, I feel like I'm going to snap." I could see small beads of sweat appearing on his body and no doubt mine as he fucked me.

Killian stopped for a moment and took a deep breath. He pulled out and I whined at the loss of being filled by him. He quickly moved us into a new position. I was straddling him, and he slipped right back inside of me. I wrapped myself around him, moving my hips that had Killian digging his fingers into my hips, guiding me to go faster and deeper.

"There we go, good girl." He praised me, and my heart skipped a bit. Being praised came from always wanting to please people and I had never wanted to please anyone more than Killian in my life. I wanted to make him feel good and in return that would make me feel good.

He reached behind me and unhooked my bra, I removed my arms from the straps. Killian took advantage of my tits being close to his face by taking one in his hands and putting my nipple into his mouth. He sucked hard and used his teeth to set my nerves alive with a sharp but enjoyable pain. He moved onto the next but used his spare hand to roll the swollen nipple between his fingers. I was losing my rhythm from the pleasure that was making my entire body feel like it was floating. Killian looked up at me with my nipple in his mouth, his eyes were glimmering with mischief. He removed his mouth and planted another kiss on my lips, giving me a chance to gain my rhythm back riding him. My sensitive nipples were pressed against his chest as we kissed.

His breath was beginning to become unsteady, moans of his own escaping his lips.

"I'm going to fill you up, Presley. You're going to get into bed with my cum leaking from your tight pretty pussy, and wish you were waking up beside me so I could clean you up with my tongue." He whispered in my ear. I moaned as he pushed himself up further into me causing me to jolt against him.

"Please, cum inside me. I need you to fill me."

"You're such a good girl aren't you, love? My perfect doting stew." He cooed as I rode him. "Don't think this will be the first and last time we will be doing this Presley, I plan on fucking you on every part of this yacht. So every room I walk into I can remember fucking you and walk around with a hard on because of it." Killian grabbed my hair in his fist and pulled my head back, stretching my body out in front of him. He balanced himself with his other hand and fucked me hard.

There was no attempt to hide my moans and screams anymore, they were being carried on the wind. The knot in my stomach was like nothing I had felt before in the position we were in. A different kind of pressure built inside of me, something I had never felt before.

"Relax for me." He ordered softly, and I tried my best to relax, letting my body move in time with his. The force of his thrusts made my tits move too, where his eyes flickered between my face and my tits.

The pressure in my core was uncontrollable and so powerful that I screamed into the night sky as I came. Unexpected wetness flooded over Killian and I. I panicked for a moment, trying to climb off of him but he fisted my hair tighter and growled at me. Seconds after I felt the warm squirts shooting up inside of me. Killian filled me to the brim with his cum and the feeling was euphoric. I was out of breath, and felt exhausted.

Killian let go of my hair and pulled me closer to him, cradling me in his arms.

"I can't believe you squirted on me. Fuck. I wish I lived on this boat." He mumbled and lay us down on the day bed, holding me.

I was beginning to regain my senses, thinking about what the fuck I had done. I swallowed, feeling disgusted with myself. I buried myself into Killian's neck, wanting to curl up and die of stupidity. I could feel his cum leaking from my pussy, the wetness drying in the cold breeze. I needed to shower and I knew I couldn't do that until the morning because May would be sleeping. I'd probably lose my job in the morning, I'd crossed a line.

"Presley stop." Killian kissed the top of my head. I looked up at him. "This won't have any effect on your job. I don't give a shit. I'm the one who has control over what I do with my boat."

"If the crew finds out-" I started.

"The crew won't, but if they do, it will be handled."

"These covers need changing." I sat up, knowing that they had a mixture of squirting, sweat and cum over them.

"I'll do it. Go sleep." He reached to brush the hair away from my face. A small smile danced on my lips.

"No, you're a guest, on your own boat. I'm meant to be looking after you." I told him.

"Believe me, love. I am very happy with the service I have received. Go to sleep, so I can see you rested tomorrow before I leave. I want to know you're okay." He seemed to really care. I tilted my head because I didn't expect him to actually care about me. I thought he was taking advantage of how horny I was, how horny we both were.

"Are you sure?"

"Positive." He sat up and kissed me lightly on the forehead. It wasn't the type where he was friend-zoning me, it was caring. He brushed my hair back and twirled it, sending a shiver down my back.

"Okay." I reached for my bra and hooked myself back into it, leaving the straps off. Then stood to grab the rest of my clothes. I quickly put them back, looking over at Killian who had stripped the day bed and got out the spare cover from the nook where the deck crew kept them.

He walked over to his watered-down whiskey, downed with the cover under his arm.

"I'll put this in the laundry?"

"Thank you, I'll do it anyway so no one will know."

Killian followed me down to the crew mess quietly and dumped the cover in the washing machine. Before I walked down the small aisle to the cabins, he grabbed my wrist and pulled me in for a quick kiss.

"Thank you for tonight, and your cocktail skills were amazing, everyone was impressed. I'll be making sure that's used this season." He whispered.

"Thank you, Killian."

"Go to bed, I'll see you in the morning. Goodnight, Love."

"Goodnight." I whispered back with a big smile on my face. I walked down to my cabin door and looked back to see Killian disappear upstairs.

I climbed into my tiny top bunk, feeling slightly gross with the mixture that was between my legs but also completely content and happy. I fell asleep quickly, exhausted from the sea air and fucking my boss.

chapter seven

I WAS THE HAPPIEST woman alive when I climbed into the shower and was able to wash away the dried cum between my legs. Luckily my hair didn't need washing, which gave me more time to sit down and eat breakfast.

I sat down in the crew mess, shovelling cereal into my mouth. Ben, one of the deckhands came down to eat breakfast too.

"How was your first night on service?" He asked, sitting down with a croissant.

"It was really good." I spoke covering my mouth because I still had some bran flakes in my mouth. "I enjoyed it. Killian and his friends are so nice."

"They are, those are usually the people that come with him, there's a couple of people that join him sometimes, but mainly those guys." I went to open my mouth to reply when the radio went off.

"Presley, Presley, Xavier." My heart stopped beating and I picked up my radio to reply.

"Go ahead for Presley." I answered.

"Can you meet me on the bridge please?"

"Of course." I answered and shoved one last spoon into my mouth, before getting up.

I walked into the bridge, ready to be told that cameras had caught me fucking Killian last night.

"You wanted to see me, Captain?" I spoke. Xavier turned around dressed in his whites with his arms folded.

"Killian came to see this morning." I felt sick to my stomach and must have looked as white as a ghost. "Don't look so afraid, Presley. He spoke to me about how well you handled last night service on your own, and how great your drinks were." My heart started beating steadily again. "I'm really proud of how well you've handled everything so far. I know you've been having some troubles with Eve and we threw you into the deep end with service last night."

"I was happy to do it, sir. I really enjoyed it."

"I'm glad, I'll make sure you'll get some more opportunities to do it again. Alcohol always goes down well with our guests. You can return to whatever you were doing. I just wanted to make sure you were praised for your work."

"Thank you, Captain." I bowed my head and headed back down to the crew mess.

I stepped into the laundry using my initiative to clean the cover and wash away the evidence of what I did last night.

"Presley, Presley, Jameson. Can I get your help in the Galley please?"

"Sure on my way," I answered and skipped upstairs to help Jameson.

"What do you need?" I asked as I strolled into the galley to help him.

"Can you chop the salad for me please, girlie?" He looked over his shoulder. "Killian asked if he could have lunch aboard, so it's all a little last minute."

"Oh yeah, of course." I grabbed the metal bowl where he had separated the salad veg. "Can I use one of your fancy knives?" I gave him a little nudge with my hip and he stuffed some pasta shells. He chuckled at me.

"Help yourself." I turned around and grabbed one of his knives from the metal strip. I preferred being able to use a super sharp knife to make it quicker. "Just please don't chop your finger off."

"I won't." I yawned, taking myself to the spare counter space to begin chopping. I took all the veg from the bowl so I could use the bowl when I had chopped it up.

"Late night?" He asked.

"Not really," I answered quickly. I was utterly fucked and I hadn't been in a while, my whole body was protesting. "Still getting used to sleeping on a boat."

I was chopping up tomatoes for Jameson when Eve strolled into the Galley.

"What are you doing?" She asked. I wanted to roll my eyes but instead, I put a smile on my face.

"She's being my sous chef." Jameson answered. I didn't need Jameson to save me every time Eve came around but it was helpful because Eve was shit scared of our Chef. Which surprised me because Jameson had been nothing but sweet to me.

"If you're not going to be long then you can sort out Killian's latte for me."

"Sure. Does he take sugar?"

"No." Eve shook her head and grabbed the bowls of nuts that were sitting on the side, then left the room.

"I wonder how stupid she can be sometimes. He takes two sugars in his latte." Jameson told me. My mouth dropped, I just couldn't understand why she was trying to set me up.

"Why does she hate me?" I sighed, sliding the tomatoes into the bowl. Jameson leaned down and put his pasta dish in the oven, then leaned beside me on the counter.

"Okay, so Eve joined the crew about five years ago. And like any person with eyes she liked the look of Captain. On rare occasions Captain joins us on a night out and she tried it on with him, he rejected her. Then he goes and hooks up with a charter guest that was still in Italy. Since then she's been crazy, when any new girls join the bottom and she thinks they have the hots for him, it's game over."

"I don't have hots for the Captain." I lied. I'd found myself looking at the Captain a little too long when I got glimpses of him but Killian seemed to be at the forefront of my mind. I was itching to see him again after last night.

"Uh, sure sweetie, you don't have hots for Cap and I'm a straight boy." He chuckled and rolled his eyes. "Anyway, I cottoned onto her plan after the last girl left the boat because of a mental breakdown, it's why I've got your back."

"Thank you." I smiled and rested my head on his shoulder. "Well I'm all done. So I'm going to make that latte for Killian."

"Go make sure you're his new favourite stew honey." I wish I could tell him that I think I already was with the way he had his face buried in my pussy on the sun deck last night.

"On it." I smiled.

My stomach was churning about seeing Killian again after last night. There was a smile on my face that I was trying to keep buried while I made his coffee. Maybe I took it one step too far though when I made a heart with the steamed milk. I kept the heart covered as I walked through the boat to the master cabin.

I inhaled and exhaled deeply before knocking on his door.

"Come in." He called from the other side of the door. I opened the door and walked in with his coffee. Killian was sitting in the armchair, shirtless and wearing cream-tailored trousers. He was wearing glasses to read from his Ipad in his lap. When he saw me, he plastered a smirk on his face.

"Shut the door, love." I did as I was asked and then walked towards him with his coffee. I placed it on the small side table beside his chair. I didn't have a moment to speak before I was pulled down into his lap. I was wearing my skirt again, giving Killian the opportunity to run his hand up my thigh and kiss my neck.

"Stop." I whispered, looking towards the door. Killian grabbed my chin and forced me to look into his dark green eyes.

"You don't get to tell me what to do, I thought you were my good girl." He spoke to me.

"We shouldn't have done what we did last night."

"How many times do I need to tell you that you don't need to worry." He sighed. He looked hot in glasses and I was disappointed when he took them off and placed them down with his Ipad beside the latte.

"I'm not worrying. I just feel as if I need to stay professional and keep my head clear."

"Your head will be clear. I won't be around all season and I know you will do a brilliant job. This thing between us is our business and it won't affect your work in the slightest, but you're mine now Presley and I don't let what's mine leave so easily." He cupped my jaw and kissed me. I wanted to melt against him and I almost did. A small hum of pleasure escaped my lips. He pulled away from me.

"Let me see, give me some time to think. Please." I whispered.

"Have your time, love. But I promised you last night that I was going to fuck you all over this boat, so you best go before I bend you over that bed and fuck you hard enough that you won't be able to walk, because you look far too comfortable today." I held my breath and nodded, standing to get some space between us, before I let him. I licked my lips tasting him on them as I walked towards the door.

I stood on the deck as Xavier and Killian spoke in the corner and his friends said goodbye to the rest of the crew. My eyes were on him. He had been on my mind for the remainder of the morning. I'd gotten into a situation that I didn't know how to get out of and I didn't want to. Every time I thought about him I thought about the way he had control over my body, the way his cock stretched me out on the sun deck. My underwear was soaked, I was walking around almost dripping because of him and I couldn't tell him, because I was doing my best at being professional.

Killian handed over a stack of cash to Xavier which he pocketed.

"Bonus on top of bonus." May whispered in my ear. I giggled and rolled my eyes at her as Killian and Xavier walked over.

"Thank you all for your perfect service as always, I wish you all the best for the rest of the charter and I will come see you all as soon as I can. I've left a little something with Xavier and I will be covering your bill for your night off tonight. So Pheonix can you grab the tabs and send me the receipts as normal?"

"Happy to, Sir."

"I bet you are." Killian chuckled. "I'll see you all soon, bye." Killian took a glance at me before he walked off the boat. Once his feet were back on the dock, the crew relaxed. I watched him walk away, pulling out his phone and making a call as he climbed into the taxi with his friends.

"Earth to Pres." May waved her hand in front of my face.

"Sorry, daydreaming."

"We've all daydreamed about Killian." Jameson put his arm around my shoulder.

"Okay crew, I want as much as you can do in the next two hours then you can all clock off for the night," Xavier called out. We all replied with 'Yes, Captain.' "Come and see me for your tip once you're free and I hope you all have a good night." Captain Xavier walked up the next steps I guessed to return to the bridge.

"Presley, we have work to do, come on." Eve snipped. I huffed and pulled myself away from Jameson.

I was already sick of cleaning cabins, constantly stripping beds, putting on the new sheets, cleaning tiles and emptying bins. With no guests to bump into I plugged in one of my AirPods with my radio in my other ear like the night Killian came back to his cabin. Music made me work quicker and the quicker we got everything done, the sooner we could relax. My phone pinged from my back pocket.

'**It's Killian. I miss my good girl already. I hope you're okay love**' My heart skipped a beat and I smiled but I didn't reply. I was a stewardess and told myself surely he couldn't have been serious about wanting me when he was a millionaire, probably billionaire. There were girls probably lined up that he wanted. Part of me was afraid that I'd just made myself an easy target, but at least I got some good sex from it. The other part was questioning why would he text me, if he didn't actually care.

My head was spinning and I locked my phone. I slipped it back into my pocket then carried on with my cleaning duties. I couldn't handle thinking.

chapter eight

"Presley. Why aren't you dressed? We're leaving in ten minutes." Jameson stood in my cabin doorway as May stuck on her eyelashes. She looked over her shoulder.

"She's not coming."

"Not coming?" Jameson looked at me. "Why aren't you coming?"

"I'm exhausted. I'm going to call home and then try and get some sleep before the she-devil works me to the bone." I told them.

"You can't miss the first night out." He folded his arms and shook his head.

"I promise I'll be out for the next one and you'll wish I had stayed back on the boat." I smiled. Jameson kissed the top of my head in his brotherly way.

"There's ice cream in the fridge. And leftover pasta too. Do you want me to make you some garlic butter for some bread quickly?" I grinned.

"I would love that. Only if you don't mind though."

"Course I don't. Got to look after my girlie haven't I?"

"Why are you never this nice to me?" May huffed.

"Because you just help yourself no matter what I'd tell you. Our Pres is a goody two shoes." Jameson left the cabin and May grabbed her shoes.

"I'll try not to be loud when I come in." She told me.

"Don't worry about it, have a good night, okay? Have a few shots for me."

"With Killian buying, there'll be more than a few." She winked and left the cabin, shutting the door behind her.

After everyone had left I took the opportunity to spend some time on the boat alone. As long as I didn't make any mess then no one would mind. I found the pasta and some garlic bread ready to be grilled, pulling myself together some dinner with the leftovers the Jameson had left me. Then I took my dinner to the main salon.

My mom said my love for cocktails came from making smoothies when I was younger, and my love for making smoothies came from stirring my ice cream together until

I made ice cream soup when I was little. I had it relaxing and when I didn't have guests throwing orders or watching me I enjoyed taking my time making cocktails. Between mouthfuls of my pasta, I used some of the leftover passion fruit to make myself a pornstar martini, made with cheap vodka rather than the top shelf stuff. I sat myself on the barstool and basked in the peace. I propped my phone up against one of the bottles and played a movie on my phone while I ate and drank.

"Not joining the others?" I jumped at the voice and held my hand against my chest, making sure my heart was still there. Captain Xavier was in the main salon dressed in a casual grey t-shirt and a pair of matching grey joggers. I cursed myself for being such a slut by looking there a little longer than I should have.

"I didn't feel up to it. Headache." I lied. He nodded.

"Do you mind if I join you?"

"Of course not." I smiled. Captain Xavier sat on the bar stool beside me.

"I don't blame you for not going out, it seems like you have the perfect set up." He nodded towards my food and cocktail. I giggled and shrugged.

"When in Italy, eat Jameson's pasta." I joked, taking another bite.

"He does have skills when it comes to carbs I find. I put on a stone when he first joined the boat because everything tasted so good."

"I have the feeling that's going to happen to me. And if it does I'll throw him overboard." I took a sip of my cocktail.

"May I taste? Killian has me curious about these skills of yours." I passed him my glass and watched his full lips wrap around the edge to take a sip. He moaned and closed his eyes to saviour it.

"Now that is perfect. Will you make me one?" He passed back my glass and I slipped off my stool. "Please finish your dinner first."

"It's okay. I'm only picking at it now anyway." I brushed off, I wanted to impress the Captain in case Eve was trying to make me lose my job.

Captain Xavier watched my every move as I made his drink. I put the lid on the shaker and pulled out a glass.

"Okay, are you ready?" I asked. "Don't laugh if this goes everywhere." I joked. I always warned people before just in case I did drop the ball for once. I was terrible at tricks when I first started at the bar in Uni.

"Carpet cleaning is coming out of your paycheck." He raised a brow. "No pressure." I took a deep breath and threw the shaker up in the air catching it with my other hand and then spun it around my body, finishing off with a couple of average shakes. I pulled off the lid and poured the cocktail into a fresh glass, sliding the foamy orange liquid filled glass to the Captain.

"Killian was praising you for your hard work." Part of me felt guilty, that I didn't really deserve the praise I was getting because I'd let him take advantage of my attraction to him.

"Just doing my job." I smiled softly and sat back down, shovelling my mouth with food so that I wouldn't speak.

"What's on your mind Presley?' Captain Xavier sighed. If I told him there was a chance I could lose my job. Maybe I wasn't cut out for the yacht life. I could go back home, find some bar work and save until I knew what I wanted to do.

I placed my fork down in my bowl and took a big gulp of my drink, before looking at Captain Xavier.

"I completely understand that I will lose my job after I tell you this but I can't carry on with the season knowing I've broken such a major rule." Xavier raised his eyebrow at me.

"Which is?"

"I slept with Killian on the Sky Deck." I spewed out of my mouth and shut my eyes, ready for the bollocking that I deserved.

"You lasted 24 hours, I'm disappointed you didn't come to me in the morning." I opened my eyes. Captain Xavier was hard to read, in fact impossible. "I'm aware of your activities, Presley. Killian and I are foremost best friends, and he came to me this morning, told me what had happened and ensured that your job was safe. Killian is our employer what he says goes. He merely told me in case the crew found out and he wanted to make sure you had someone keeping an eye out for you."

"So my job is really safe?" I whispered. The weight off my shoulders was lifted.

"Your job is yours, Presley. Don't worry yourself, my sweet." Captain Xavier stood. "And don't let it stop you from bonding with your crew. Thank you for the beverage." He raised his glass.

"Thank you, Captain. And I promise it won't happen again." Xavier smiled and leant down to whisper in my ear.

"If it does happen again, I'd suggest being a little quieter. Or I'll suggest to Killian he gag you, who knows who else could have heard." He looked me in the eye, our faces so close to one another. And for a split second I wanted to see if Captain Xavier tasted like the sea he sailed on.

I was left speechless as Captain Xavier left the salon.

I was beyond mortified that my Captain had heard me moaning during sex, surprised that I had been that loud. Although his suggestion of me being gagged left a small wet patch on my underwear that I had managed to avoid for a couple of hours.

chapter nine

'I'M OKAY. I'M SORRY I just needed a moment to think. I don't want to text too much in case the crew think something weird is going on.' I finally replied back to Killian. I dropped my phone on the bed and chewed on my fingernails waiting for a reply.

'I'll take whatever I'm given. I'll be back in three weeks.' I picked up my phone to reply back to him.

'Captain heard us.'

'I know he suggested I gag you next time.' My cheeks blushed red, he'd told Killian the same thing. I was starting to get the feeling that Captain Xavier had a secret kinky lifestyle no one knew about.

I had a big smile on my face when May walked out of the shower, wrapping a towel around herself.

"What are you smiling at?" She asked.

"Nothing. Just a friend telling me a story about a date back home." The lie rolled off my tongue and added extra weight to the secret I was already hiding from her. May was beginning to be one of my closest friends. It was bound to happen when we lived in such a small space together.

I thought it was going to be an easy day, a lot had been done the day before but Eve was still trying to prove her point. Do this, do that. It was understandable because she was my boss, but I knew she was just trying to wear me down to the bone so I'd mess up at some point. It only pushed me further to complete every task she gave me to the highest of standards.

My heart hadn't touched a resting heart rate in hours, I had sweat running down my forehead and the only moments I had to grab a drink were when I passed the galley and took a quick swig of the water bottle Jameson left on the side for me. Eve was sitting in the main dining room, sorting out provisions and I hadn't seen Chessa in a few hours, so I had no idea what she was doing. It was like Eve's goal was to rearrange the whole boat again before the next charter.

I was out of breath as I stopped in the galley again. Jameson threw his tea towel down on the counter and his face was red with fury.

"I'm not fucking taking this. You're a Third Stew, not a fucking slave." He growled, picking up his radio. "Eve, Eve, James." He tried his best not to sound pissed off, as I down some more water.

"Go ahead."

"I'm going into town for provisions later and I'll be taking Pres with me." Eve never replied which I thought was unusual. It was less than a minute later though when Eve strolled into the kitchen.

"Presley is busy, can you take Chessa?" She folded her arms.

"No. I'm taking Presley, because she needs a break from you. All morning you've had her running around like a maniac while you nurse your hangover. She's not your fucking slave."

"She's my stew and I'm her boss. If Presley can't handle it then she can talk to me." There was no way that I could talk to Eve. She was insane and hated me. I only did what she asked to prove a point but I was burning out. Jameson put his hands on my shoulders and directed me to the walk in fridge, pulling open the door.

"Cool down, girlie." He ordered. Locking us both in there. I let out a small laugh.

"Think she'll still be out there when we get out?" I asked. The temperature of the fridge was already doing a great deal of cooling me down.

"Nah, she'll sprout some shit to Pheonix and the deck crew making out that I bullied her. She'll cry. Cap will console her then give me a 'warning'." He quoted with his fingers. "Cap knows she's a two face bitch. But you stay in here, cool down and then go get showered. I want to head to some local butchers for this charter and get inspired."

"Sounds great, thanks James."

I took one of the longest cold showers I possibly could. I quickly braided my hair rather than drying it, thinking that the dampness would help keep me cool while we walked around. I put my spare blues back on, pairing with a pair of shorts, thinking that even though we were going to town I was still on the clock. Although working with Jameson was a lot more peaceful than running around after crazy Eve.

I opened my cabin door and jumped back when I saw that exact person standing on the other side of it.

"If you have a problem with the way I manage you, then talk to me rather than getting the Chef to fight your battles."

"I don't ask him to fight my battles. I can fight on my own. But if someone else is calling you out for being a bitch then maybe you should listen." I shoved past her and stormed up the stairs to the galley. Jameson was waiting for me while playing on his phone.

"Get me off this boat." I begged. He looked up and slipped his phone away,

"Please don't tell me she went down there to corner you." Jameson huffed.

"Yeah, but I'm fine. Let's go."

Getting off the boat for a couple of hours was just what I needed. Jameson had ordered from various fishmongers and butchers, hand-picking each dish. I'd got my mom and Aunt Marie some tacky keychains.

"Fancy getting some food?" Jameson asked.

"Please, I am starved." I linked arms with him as we strolled towards the Pizzeria on the other side of the path.

"We went to one of the prettiest restaurants last night, you should have come with us." He told me.

"I'll be there next time. I just needed some alone time." Which had turned into being embarrassed by the Captain. I considered for a moment to tell Jameson about everything. I need someone to talk to and the only other people that I trusted were May, Mom, and Auntie Marie. But my family were known to be a little judgey over the years, and I didn't want to put May in that position. At least Jameson was higher up the chain of command, but I hadn't known him long so I didn't know how much I should have trusted him with.

Jameson and I returned back to the boat just in time for everyone to go get dinner. I put my best foot forward. I told myself that I would try my best to dive into the group and get to know everyone a little better.

"Pres! Grab another bottle of white!" May called over the music from the crew mess. Even with a charter arriving tomorrow, everyone was keen on going out again.

"Okay!" I shouted back down. I spun into the pantry where I had made a jug of sex on the beach and grabbed another bottle of white from the fridge, still dancing to the music I could faintly hear.

"I'm glad you're having fun." Captain Xavier was standing in the galley holding a wrapped plate that Jameson had probably prepared for him.

"Thank you." I'd managed to avoid the Captain all day in case he changed his mind about firing me.

I stepped past him and he called my name softly. I turned back around, realising he had stepped closer. There were inches between us, I was close enough I could make out every single beard hair along with his sea blue eyes. He was truly handsome, and if I hadn't already fucked up maybe I would have crossed a different line. Just like I had wanted to last night.

"If I upset you with my words last night, Presley, it wasn't my intention."

"I don't think I'm in much of a position to complain. What I did was wrong. I know that. It won't happen again, so your suggestion is redundant."

"Maybe or maybe not. Enjoy your night, my sweet. Remember you can come talk to me anytime." The Captain smiled at me, and walked off towards the bridge. I shook myself down and jogged down to the crew mess where everyone was getting ready.

Maybe or maybe not. Even the Captain knew I wasn't strong enough to resist Killian. Or even him. And that made me a bigger slut.

chapter ten

I WAS FILLED WITH bruschetta and steak, and I'd drank way too much wine to get through the night of Eve giving me the cold shoulder. Luckily I'd had everyone else who had made the night enjoyable. No one had stayed up when we got back, we were all exhausted and ready for bed. While my body felt every bit tired, my brain was running around in circles and I couldn't fall asleep. I grabbed my hoodie from the bottom of my bunk and slipped off my bed. Carefully I left the cabin where May was snoring her head off.

I pulled my hoodie over my head and wrapped my arms around myself. Despite it being the summer, once I had gotten used to the heat, I felt the cold at night.

We were docked, so there was no one on anchor watch, meaning I could go watch the stars from the bridge until

I was tired. I thought about going to watch them on deck but it would have been cold.

I carefully opened the door to the bridge, my eyes on the cabin door that belonged to the Captain. I should have reconsidered going out on the deck because the bridge wasn't empty, Captain Xavier was sitting in his chair, shirtless, and it was too late for me to back out. He turned around facing me directly and I tried to speak. It wasn't like we weren't allowed on the bridge, I was just taken back by his presence. He was just as stunningly beautiful as Killian. Two best friends that were sculpted with clay for women.

Xavier's presence was like the sea he adored so much, a soothing wave until the storm hit. I knew that just underneath the surface there was a dominant man, even if he was a calm captain. He suggested gagging me, and that made me think that's what he wanted to do to me. Last time I made a mistake I was sober. This time I was drunk and I suspected I'd make a worse one.

"I couldn't sleep." I swallowed. "Is it okay to watch the stars up here?" I hiccuped, the wine had finally hit me. I hiccuped again, earning a little chuckle from Xavier.

"More than welcome, my sweet." I walked towards the control panel and wheel to look out of the window, trying to keep my distance. My hiccups kept going and already getting frustrating. "Did you enjoy your night?"

"It was good." I rushed out before another hiccup hit me. "May and I drank a lot of wine." I admitted.

"Remind me to make her work harder tomorrow then." He smirked. I hiccuped and smiled back at him in my tipsy dazed state. I looked back out the window trying to spot the stars. They were much easier to see when we anchored out at sea. "Here." He switched the bridge lights off. The only lighting in the room was from the control panel.

I hiccuped again.

"Sorry." I quickly glanced at him, then tried to hold my breath. I failed, the hiccups still happening.

"Come here." Xavier nudged me over. I took a few steps closer to him, still trying to keep some sort of distance. He passed me a glass of water and I took the biggest mouthful I could while holding my breath. I passed the glass back to him. My hiccups seemed to have gone and I sighed in relief.

"Thank you." Although my peace was short-lived, I hiccuped again. Captain Xavier chuckled at me.

"Maybe next time you should stick to cocktails rather than wine." I nodded.

"You're right." I hiccuped. Xavier reached out to me and pulled me so I was standing in front of him in his chair.

"Okay, the water didn't work. Let's try something else."

"Like what?" I hiccuped again.

"Surprise." He answered.

I didn't have time to process what was happening, but it did surprise me. Captain Xavier's lips were on mine, and I kissed him back in return. It was a distraction for my brain. And it did stop my hiccups, but it also made my stomach churn. Killian crossed my mind and a wave of guilt came crashing down on me. At the same time, my mind wondered why he was kissing me when he knew that Killian had fucked me a couple of days ago. He had heard me being fucked, and they were best friends.

I pulled away, pressing myself against the wheel. Xavier was leaning forward in his chair.

"How sober are you?" He whispered.

"Quite, the hiccups always come after." That was all it took for Xavier to kiss me again, biting down on my lip and claiming me in a different way to Killian. He was powerful rather than gentle. He knew what he wanted and he was going to have it. What he wanted was me. Xavier pulled me into his lap. I got comfortable on his lap, my legs swung to the side and my hands wrapped in his curly blonde hair. I was undeniably going to hell after.

"You're wearing too many clothes." He mumbled against my lips. I giggled, and pulled back to pull my hoodie off leaving me in a vest top and my cycling shorts. My nipples were against the white fabric and even in the low lighting you could see how perky they were. Xavier twirled my hair around his finger and took a moment to admire me, which made my heart pound. "Did Killian treat you gently?" He asked.

"Partially." I answered, thinking back to the way his fist was wrapped in my hair as he fucked himself up into me.

"I was jealous. Hearing you moan for him, when I wanted it to be me." I blushed. I couldn't understand how I ended up in the position where I had two men, who could have any women in the world and they wanted me.

"Then see if you can make me moan too."

Captain Xavier took the opportunity to pull my tits from my vest. Taking my nipples between his fingers and using my nipples to tug me closer to him. I whined in pain, but even if I was in pain, my pussy was sending a whole different message.

"Be careful what you wish for." He smirked. "I'm going to take you right here on the bridge, my sweet girl." My entire body shivered.

"Take me, before I come to my senses and get myself the hell off this boat." I whispered.

"Get on your knees." I stood and kneeled beside the chair for more room. Xavier spun to face me, lifting his hips to pull down his trousers. He threw them to the side and I looked at the doors to make sure we were alone. "No one will be up for hours, you don't need to worry. Now put that mouth to good use."

I turned back to see the long length that was in my direct eyesight. Xavier was longer than Killian, and almost the same girth. The head of his cock was red and already dripping pre-cum that ran down Xavier's hand that was holding it off his stomach. I placed my hands on his knees, and pulled myself up to reach the pretty head that was begging to be sucked on.

Xavier pulled in a sharp breath as soon as my lips touched his cock. I swallowed as much of his cock as I could, struggling with the length. What I couldn't fit in my mouth I used my hands. Starting slow I bobbed my head, and used my tongue underneath the head. Touching the sensitive skin there, I had Xavier shuddering. I smiled to myself as much as I could with my mouth filled. I looked up, my eyes locking with his. Xavier was holding back on me, the look in his eyes told me he was holding onto the last bit of self control he had. I moved fast, each time managing to swallow a little bit more of his cock, but I couldn't bring myself to take the last inch knowing that I would gag if I did.

Xavier finally made a move to touch me. His hand gently touched my head, as if he was stroking my hair. In the next second, his hand was wrapped in my short blonde hair as he forced me to move faster on him. I hollowed my cheeks around his cock, my mouth was almost as tight as what my pussy was. Xavier's grip loosened for a moment, losing his senses from the moans that were coming out of his mouth.

"You're a fucking devil in disguise." He mumbled. "Suck harder." He ordered and I did my best with how numb my mouth was. I wanted to make Xavier feel a level of pleasure that he had never had before.

I jumped back when Xavier stood, giving me a new angle to suck him off. What I didn't expect was him to force my head down to the base of his cock. I gagged around him which made him praise me further. He let go of my hair and

I pulled myself from him, s string of saliva running from my lips to his tip. He smiled down on me as I coughed.

"I didn't tell you to stop, my sweet girl." He smirked and pushed my head lightly back towards him.

I placed him in my mouth again, saliva beginning to drip down my chin as I fucked my mouth on him, using my tongue to make his balls tighten.

"I'm going to cum in that pretty little mouth of yours Presley, and you best swallow every last drop." He pushed his hips forward in an attempt to make me gag on his thick cock. "Then I'm going to fuck you." Xavier was harsher than Killian but part of me enjoyed it. Killian was sensual and Xavier wanted it messy. "Use your tongue." He mumbled, closing his eyes to hide from the sensitivity around his cock.

I hollowed my cheeks as much as possible, swirling my tongue and bobbing my head faster. With my hands braced on his thighs I could feel his muscles clenched meaning he was so close. Within seconds hot cum was filling my mouth and spilling down my throat. I looked Xavier in the eye as I swallowed every last drop, pulling away from him, I licked my lips.

His fingers traced my jaw with a satisfied smile on his face, as he sat down in his chair. I don't know what the man ate to still be at half-mast but he was gently resting against his stomach. He pushed his damp hair back, his chest moving rapidly, the sound of his breath the only sound in the room. He gestured for me to come to him, I stood, wiping my mouth with the back of my hand and taking a step towards him.

Xavier put his hand forward, dragging a finger over my wet pussy. I shivered, Xavier had neglected touching me so far. It was like an itch that I needed scratching. I whimpered as his finger brushed over my clit.

"You're a good little slut aren't you my sweet girl." He tilted his head as he rubbed my clit in circles. I nodded and moaned, the vibrations aching my sore jaw.

"Yes." I mumbled.

"Come closer." He ordered. I took another step towards him and he spun me around to sit on his lap, his wet cock touching my back. He pulled me to lean against him, and turned my head.

He closed his eyes as he pushed our lips together. Kissing Xavier reminded me of the fresh sea salt air, like he was giving me a fresh breath of life. I lifted my hand to cup his stubbled cheek as our lips moved against one another, hungry for more. His other hand rested on my bare waist. I could feel him growing harder by the second and I didn't quite know how he was going to go for another round, and manage to fill my pussy like he promised.

We pulled away from one another and pressed our foreheads together to take a breath.

"Do you want me to fuck you from the front or from the back?" He whispered.

"Back." I had always found that getting bent over and being fucked caused a man to turn primal when fucking. I stood and looked down at his cock ready to perform again.

Xavier changed our position, bending me over the chair and him standing behind me. He held open my ass cheeks and I looked over my shoulder to watch him looking down as he pushed himself inside of me. I grasped the chair and moaned at the feeling of being filled again.

I don't know how I'd ended up in a position where I was being fucked by someone that shouldn't be fucking me. There was something about being fucked by your superior that I was beginning to enjoy, even though I should have run a thousand miles and headed straight back home.

Xavier started off with a slow pace, pressing his pelvis tightly against my ass. With every thrust I moaned, my eyes rolling into the back of my head, as I let myself drown in the euphoria I was given. Xavier changed his pace, thrusting into me with a sharp flick of his hips and tilting my ass up to reach the exact spot that would have me crying out and screaming for him in a few moment's time.

He slowly pulled out of me, to the tip, and thrusted back into me with a sharp motion. Holding myself up was a struggle, my legs were shaking and Xavier used it to his advantage as his thrusts became manic and he used me like the slut he had called me.

"Fuck me. Harder." I begged, though I wasn't quite sure how much harder he could fuck me when his balls were slapping against my pussy. I tried to cover my mouth with my forearm, screaming into my skin, in case we woke anyone. But the harder I was fucked, the more I lost my senses and I wanted to moan at the top of my lungs.

Xavier pulled out in a swift motion and turned me around. I squealed when he picked me up and placed me on top of his cock, the new angle sending a shiver down my spine as I held onto him. I was surprised by his strength as he bounced me up and down. I buried my face in his neck, my lips against the sensitive skin. Lost in the pleasure I was feeling, I bit down on the base of his neck, trying to hold back the knot in my stomach. The sensation almost overwhelmed me. Xavier growled, his fingers digging into my ass. I bit harder, and I knew I'd have left marks on him that he would struggle to hide.

"I'm never going to stop fucking you, my sweet girl." He moaned, sitting me down on the cold table where he had preference sheet meetings. Where he would sit tomorrow and remember how he fucked me on the table.

I was laid back on the cold wood and fucked on my back. I gasped as he wrapped his hand around my throat. I smiled at him, dazed. Xaviers thrusts were getting sloppier and I could tell he was close to filling my pussy just like he had my mouth.

"Hold it." He ordered. "We're finishing together, or I'll spank your ass raw." Xavier's breath was heavy and uneven, groaning between his words as he was holding back. But I was doing the same. I was dying to clench around his cock and soak it like I had Killian's. I nodded the best I could with his hand around my throat.

"I need to cum." I moaned as he hit my sensitive spot, nearly sending me over the edge.

"Together. Three. Two. Cum for me." He hissed. At the same time his throbbing cock began to fill me, my pussy clenched around him as I moaned so loudly in pleasure that he had moved to cover my mouth. I put my hand over his as my entire body jolted from cumming. Once he had stopped spilling into me he pulled out and got down on his knees.

His tongue caught our mixed cum that was leaking from my pussy. I hissed from the over simulation. I was surprised that he was down there cleaning me up with his tongue. I closed my eyes and tried to calm down. Until he moved towards my clit, sucking on my hard bud. I gasped, and bit down on my knuckle to stop myself from moaning. He flicked his tongue over my clit and I could feel the ache and pressure between my legs. I knew that there was no holding back from cumming again. I relaxed my body allowing myself to revel in the pleasure.

My entire body shivered as I came again and my whole body turned weak as it pushed out the leftovers of our orgasms. Xavier finished up cleaning between my legs with his tongue before he lifted me into his arms and I was seeing stars as he held me. I limply wrapped my arm around him.

I vaguely remember being placed into a double bed pressed against the wall, knowing that I wasn't falling asleep in my own cabin.

"No." I whispered. "They'll know." As much as I protested, my body had other ideas as I curled around the equally naked body and covers were placed over us.

"I'll wake you before anyone finds out." He whispered against my hair. "Sleep, my sweet girl." My brain wanted to say no and drag myself back down stairs to my bunk, but my body was happily snuggled against the chest of my Captain, who had kept his promise of making me scream.

chapter eleven

I woke up in the arms of Captain Xavier and waited for the regrets to hit me like a wrecking ball. They didn't and that was far more concerning. Killian and Xavier were close friends and that alone was bad enough never mind being my employer and my Captain.

His arm tightened around my waist as we spooned, telling me he was awake.

"What time is it?" I mumbled.

"Seven thirty." He whispered. "No one will be awake until at least eight thirty." I rolled over and he loosened his grip on me.

We faced one another and looked into each other's eyes.

"Why?" I asked.

"Why what?"

"Why did you fuck me knowing that Killian has too? You're friends."

"One day, you'll realise exactly why I did. But for now I don't want you worrying about what we've done together. Nothing will change and during charters I am your Captain outside of that I will gladly sneak every second I can with you." I blushed and turned my head away. Xavier refused to let me shut away from him and turned my head back towards him, then placed a kiss on my lips.

"I just don't understand why you've both, or I... I fucked you both. That makes me such a slut. And I don't know why you've both let me or wanted me."

"Why can't it simply be because we can, because we want to? Don't overthink every decision you make, Presley. Else you'll never make a life-changing one in your life." I sighed and closed my eyes, trying to balance myself.

"I should go, before someone wakes up." I told him.

"Okay. I'll come find you when I can. If you're having any more problems with Eve, then please tell me."

"I'm not going to use whatever advantage I have with you to deal with Eve. She'll give in one day, or James will smash her around the head with a pan." I joked. Xavier laughed and swept back my hair, giving me another sweet kiss even if he did taste like a salty sea day.

I had to climb over Xavier to get out of bed and that was awkward in itself. I threw one leg over him and Xavier took the opportunity of me straddling him to pull me down to his lips again. I giggled and attempted to pull away.

"I need to go." I mumbled.

"Then go." He whispered, kissing me again.

"You're kind of kissing me."

"And?"

"You'll end up getting us caught." I sighed, but found myself kissing him.

"Okay. Okay." He sighed and stopped. "Go, my sweet girl." Xavier let me climb over him. I noticed my PJ's sitting on top of his desk and grabbed them. With one last look over my shoulder, I took the image of the naked man in his bed, the covers barely covering anything at all. My cheeks heated up and I closed the door behind me.

I managed to sneak downstairs to the crew mess and cabins and back into my bunk. May was still snoring away, one arm hanging off her bunk. May being a heavy sleeper was definitely the universe being on my side.

"Shit." I noticed that I was still in Xavier's t-shirt. I quickly stripped off the t-shirt and shoved it under my pillow. I grabbed my work shirt from the shelf by my porthole and pulled it over my head.

I lay in my bed and my head was spinning. So much had happened in a few short days. Killian's question floated around in my head as I thought about the time I had spent with him and Xavier. It was any girl's dream to be caught in between two stunning men wasn't it? But I wasn't sure if it was my dream.

Maybe my dream was somewhere quiet, still by the sea, close to a dock where Aunt Marie could dock up on a Charter Yacht.

I lay there thinking for too long, my alarm and May's went off at the same time and my cabin mate groaned.

"Don't tell me it's true." She fake cried.

"It is." I laughed, and poked my head underneath. May was covering her face with her arm. I reached over on the wall and turned the light switch on.

"No, why did you do that?" She whined.

"Because Phe will have your head if you're late on deck."

"I'm due a late one."

"If we get up before everyone else, maybe Jameson will make us some French toast?"

"Good point."

It was a race to get ready, both of us crammed into one space, accidentally elbowing each other. We both raced up stairs to the galley, where Jameson was already cooking. It must have heard us coming because he turned around and placed two plates on the counter. French toast and berries, which weren't cut, because that's where Jameson drew the line in making us breakfast.

"Have I ever told you I love you?" May hopped up onto the counter and grabbed her plate.

"Hmm, get your perky ass off my counter, May."

"Oh you got told." I laughed, leaning over the counter and taking a bite of my toast. May threw a blueberry at my head.

chapter twelve

I DIDN'T THINK THAT Eve could have done much worse to me then shoving me in laundry and leaving me to do turn downs on my own. But she was an evil mastermind at her best. From the moment the guests had stepped onto the boat they had been the type that took full advantage of being on a luxury yacht, and having people to wait on them hand and foot. Eve's greatest idea was to have me on dinner service and for her to do almost nothing to help.

I had a layer of sweat on my forehead, my hair had been shoved up into a bun, trying to make it look as nice as I could. I'd just cleared the main course and Jameson was finishing plating his creme brûlées, using a torch to crisp the tops. I put the plates on the side and was ready to serve the dessert when Chessa walked up the stairs looking prim and proper, after doing turn downs.

"Chessa, you need to help." Jameson ordered and put down the torch. Chessa looked at the state of me.

"Woah, what happened to you?" She asked.

"I've been on my own all service, Eve said she had a migraine and then they were requesting cocktails left right and centre. And I needed to clear and run."

"Why did you not radio anyone?" She asked.

"Because that is defeat. I grabbed Elliot when he passed." Chessa looked at Jameson who was staring her down. Chessa hadn't made things much easier for me and she was beginning to realise how determined Eve was to break me for no reason at all.

"Here. I'll help you take these up." She grabbed two plates and I grabbed another two.

"I can bring the last ones and show my face." Jameson straightened his chef jacket and followed us up to the guests who were on the aft deck for dinner.

I placed the two plates I had in my hands in front of the guests and smiled.

"For dessert, we have creme brûlée, with a side of my signature bacon ice cream." Jameson introduced and I was beyond grateful because my throat was tired after saying 'Yes of course' all day.

"Can we get another round of cosmopolitans?" The Primary Charter guest, Debbie spoke without even saying thank you.

"Yes, of course." I answered with a slight nod. "I'll go make those for you while you enjoy your dessert."

I headed back down to the galley and made the Cosmos in the stew pantry that I had made an absolute mess over after not being able to have a moment to breathe.

"Here, I'll take them up." Chessa was back at my side. I nodded.

"Yeah, please. I gotta start cleaning this up." Chessa picked up the tray and headed back to the guests. I stood leaned over the counter and took a deep breath. A hand was placed on my back and rubbed in circles. Jameson recited calming words to me as I calmed down my heart rate.

"Everything okay? What happened?" I looked up to see Captain Xavier standing in the galley.

"Rough service," Jameson answered.

I was at a breaking point, and guilt flooded me for using my new dynamic with Xavier to grass on Eve, but at the same time, he was the person I had to go to with a problem when it came to my Chief Stew.

"I just did service almost completely on my own because Eve said she had a migraine," I told him. It was hard to read his expression. Xavier took his blank face and looked at Jameson for confirmation.

"It was a shit show. She didn't call Chessa to back her up and Pres was determined to do it on her own to prove a point, but these guests are tough."

"Where's Chessa now?" Xavier asked.

"With the guests."

"Presley, clean this up and then head to bed. I'll deal with Eve in the morning. Is Chessa on lates tonight or you?"

"Chessa." I answered.

"Then that works. And are you okay?"

"Yeah, I'm fine. My head is just spinning." Those guests were nothing like how chill Killian and his friends had been. These guests thought they were entitled and I knew we were going to have guests like it. I just didn't expect it so soon into my first charter.

I cleaned up the mess I had made as quickly as I could because my bed was calling out for me. When I climbed in I moaned out loud, I reached for my phone and checked my texts.

Killian and I had been texting when I could. He'd put no pressure on me, just throwing random, silly questions that left me smiling. Yet there was a layer of guilt that was eating me alive with every secret smile that I gave Xavier as we passed one another on the boat or the secret kisses that came with his morning coffee.

It had been almost a week since Xavier had fucked me on the bridge. I'd managed to keep it to myself. I didn't have the privacy to tell friends back home and there was no way I could tell Aunt Marie without a lecture about professionalism.

There was something about the yacht that meant I could never sleep through the night. Maybe I was more homesick than I liked to admit or the bunks were nothing compared to the king size bed I had at home.

I found myself climbing down from my bunk again. Although this time around I knew that Phoenix was upstairs on anchor watch and I had to be as quiet as possible to sneak into Xavier's cabin. It was one of the biggest risks I had taken next to sleeping with my two bosses, because if there was any problem like the anchor dragging, Phoenix could barge into Xavier's cabin.

I was quick as I opened the door and slid into the room. There was a dim light coming from his bedside lamp, and Xavier was sitting in bed, shirtless, with a pair of black-rimmed glasses on his face and reading a book. The hardback was blue leather with silver script writing out 'Great Expectations'.

"Sorry, I couldn't sleep." I whispered.

"There's no need to be sorry. I'm guessing you snuck up here?" He put down his book on his bedside table and placed his glasses on top.

"Yeah, is that okay?" I stepped towards the bed, keeping my voice quiet.

"I've been wishing you would for days." I climbed onto the bed, to the side nearest the wall. The side of the bed was untouched like he had been waiting for me to appear. Almost like it was the unspoken rule that it was my side of the bed. I sat up, curled my knees up, and wrapped my arms around them.

"Are you okay after tonight? I didn't enjoy seeing you so stressed out."

"Better. I just can't seem to sleep.."

"Back when I was a deckhand, it took me almost two years to sleep through the night unless I'd had a drink."

"It's not like I can even feel the boat swaying that much, I don't know, maybe I'm more homesick than I thought I was."

"Come here." Xavier lifted the sheets up, and I climbed underneath, curling into the side of his body and letting my own finally relax. My eyes were trained on the door. Anyone could call out for the captain at any time, and there was no playing the position cool. Especially if things ended up the way they did last time.

I lifted my head to look up at Xavier, a little smirk danced on his lips, as he bent down to kiss me. His hand cupped my cheek, taking the opportunity to kiss me deeply rather than stealing fleeting kisses on coffee runs. A weak whimper escaped between my lips and Xavier chuckled as he pulled away.

"My sweet girl." He whispered. There was no questioning the depth of my blush, my cheeks were burning red but Xavier stroked my flushed skin with a smile on his face. His eyes glanced between the door and I. Then he placed another kiss on my lips.

"Do you trust me?" He whispered. I tiled my head and considered it for a moment.

"Yes."

Xavier climbed out of bed and I watched him intently as he pulled open his draw. When he turned around there was a tie in his hand. My heart beat almost out of my chest as he stepped closer. I sat up on my knees, my nerves higher than they had ever been, and I'd fucked my bosses on the sundeck and on the bridge.

"I want you, but we both know how loud you can be, my sweet girl."

"You want to gag me?" I blinked.

"Only if you want to be, or I'll have to find other ways of keeping that pretty mouth of yours quiet." He put the tie down on the bed and perched himself on the edge. He brushed my hair back from my face, wrapping it around his wrist and giving it a tug. A small gasp escaped my lips and then I laughed lightly at him.

I reached out for the tie and handed it to him.

"Hold your hair up for me?" He asked. I did as I was asked and lifted my hair as he took hold of the tie with two hands. I parted my lips so that the tie would sit comfortably in my mouth. I'd been gagged before, back in university with a guy

I was seeing, but with Xavier, it felt like a new experience. Everything with him was new, everything with Killian was new. He was still there floating in the back of my mind. I found myself wishing he was there, which only made the tension between my legs wetter. The silk tie was soft on the corners of my mouth, and Xavier tied it firmly around the back of my head. I let go of my hair and looked up at him, his hair a pile of messy curls and I could see how tired he was but at the same time he was looking at me like he wanted to devour me. I glanced down at his shorts.

From what I could remember the sight in his shorts was only half as hard as he had been that night on the bridge.

"Lay back." He ordered. I took a moment to touch the silk tie in my mouth and then lay down with my knees up. I lifted myself onto my elbows and Xavier stepped forward, his knees hitting the edge of the bed. I lifted up my hips as he reached for the waistband of my shorts. He pulled them off, throwing them onto the floor. I wasn't wearing any underwear again, but the only times I had alone time with Xavier was when I was meant to be sleeping.

"Are you like this all the time?" Xavier smirked, and dragged one of his fingers down my pussy lips, sweeping up the wetness. I watched him intently as he licked his fingers.

I was breathing heavily because of the silk tie. My insides were clenched. I regretted agreeing to be gagged because I wanted to beg him to fuck me and forget the foreplay. I attempted to plead with my eyes, but it was like Xavier could read my mind and he wasn't going to give me what I wanted. He wanted to deny me just because he could. Instead of having me on a table we were in the comfort of his bed.

He pushed two fingers directly inside of me, slipping into my tight and wanting hole. My hips bucked and I clenched down on the silk tie. Even with the tie I could hear my groans as he curled his fingers against just the right spot. He switched between thrusting his two fingers inside of me and curling them. He placed one knee on the bed and leaned over me, using his other hand to press down on my pelvis bone. The pleasure was unfounded, I was screaming against the silk and trying to pull myself up the bed to escape it. I had no luck, Xavier had me exactly where he wanted me and I was going to cum whether I liked it or not.

He chuckled lightly, his tongue swiping over his bottom lip as he pulled his fingers out. He raised them to my eye line. His fingers were dripping with the wetness between my legs.

"You're still so tight, my sweet girl. We need to fix that." He smirked, dropping his hand back down to my cunt. Except the next time he thrust his fingers into me, there were three. I cried out, my eyes watering, as he stretched me out for whatever he had planned. The pain was soothing and I closed my eyes, allowing myself to revel in the pleasure. Instinctively I lifted my hands under my vest and brushed my fingers over my nipples. I began to rub my nipples between two fingers, applying more and more pressure when I felt the waves in my stomach beginning to swell.

"Shhh, my sweet girl. Someone is going to hear you. Maybe next time I'll need to stuff your mouth to keep you quiet. Maybe your underwear…or Killian's cock." I dropped my hands and my eyes flew open in panic. "Have you told him, Presley? Told him how I fucked you in his bridge?" I shook my head. "You should." He said as he pushed another finger inside of me. I moaned as my body accommodated all four of his fingers. "He might spank you for it, but then he'd fucked you just as hard." I moaned, finding myself imagining Killian in the room with Xavier and I, fucking my mouth, fucking my pussy to take ownership of me. Both men would try to prove a point.

I could hear the wet sounds filling the room, and the knot in my stomach being pulled tighter as I gripped the bed sheets. Xavier pushed his fingers down to the knuckle. My hips bucked and I released my climax all over his hand without warning. My jaw clamped down on the wet silk tie in my mouth. He moved his hand off my pelvis and linked his hand with one of mine.

"Shh, there we go. Fuck Presley, where have you been all my life?" He whispered. I wished I could smile through the gag, my heart fluttering. "One more, then I promise to fuck you."

I thought he meant one more orgasm but no Xavier meant one more finger, or more so thumb. The orgasm lubricated his hand further and I was looser, which allowed him to push his thumb alongside the four fingers. I gasped.

"Come on, I know you can do this. Breathe for me. Relax." I closed my eyes and tried to steady my breath. As inhaled Xavier pushed past the knuckle bone and his entire fist was inside of me. I gasped, and opened my eyes to look at him. My eyes were watering and leaking down the side of my face. He let go of my hand and pulled the gag away.

"Oh my god." I whispered.

"How does that feel, my sweet girl?" He brushed my cheeks.

"I can't. I can't explain it."

"Try."

"Full." I answered. "Dirty, but in a good way."

"And how about when I do this?" Xavier curled and uncurled his hand inside of me and I moaned. I clamped my hand over my mouth in panic. He began to pull his hand out and my eyes were rolling into the back of my head out of euphoric pleasure, then he pushed in further, his wrist gaping open my pussy. "So perfect, you're a good little slut, Presley. Do you need me to fuck you?"

"Yes."

"Yes, what?" He curled his hand again and I whimpered.

"Yes, Captain."

"Good girl. Breathe and relax." He ordered. I followed my orders and once my body was relaxed enough Xavier pulled his fist from my cunt. He grabbed a towel from the back of his desk chair, quickly wiping his hand and discarding it. Xavier pulled my legs further open. It felt like an almost breeze down there.

"Fuck." He groaned as he stared at my pussy. "You're gaping, and now I'm going to fuck you and fill this gaping hole to the brim with my cum." I nodded as he pulled down his shorts.

The head of his cock was weeping and red, every vein standing out. Without warning, Xavier flipped me onto my stomach and pulled up my hips. I spread my legs. Xavier shoved my head down into the mattress.

"You scream into the mattress. If I hear you, I'll punish you." I nodded, although I wasn't sure that he could see me.

Slowly he pushed the head of his cock into me and I could hear the sigh of relief.

"I can't wait this long again, never again." He mumbled. "I'm going to fuck you every day for the rest of my life." I lifted my head to speak.

"Promise?"

"Promise, you're my sweet girl until the end now." I smiled and buried my head back into his sheets, just in time as he buried himself to the hilt in my pussy. It didn't feel as tight as before, but that didn't mean that it didn't feel just as good.

Xavier didn't take his time with fucking me, he went fast and hard. There was no mercy for the way he fucked me into his mattress. I covered my moans with the white sheets. The only sound in the room was Xavier's heavy breathing. My entire body felt sensitive, the knot tying in my stomach as he pushed me towards the edge again. Xavier stopped for a moment and I held my breath when I felt something else pushing inside of me. He had pushed two of his fingers alongside his dick to stretch me out further and I couldn't take much more of the pleasure that was radiating from my body. My legs were shaking from the pressure of holding back my orgasm as he fucked me with his cock and fingers at the same time.

"I can't hold on." I lifted my head up to speak.

"On my count." He said out of breath. There were a few more sharp thrusts before he counted. "Three, two, one. Cum for me, Presley." I was happy to oblige. My walls clenched around his hard cock as he came inside of me. Both of us took deep breaths. Xavier pulled out and I collapsed onto the bed and rolled over.

Xavier grabbed the box of tissues sitting on his side and began to clean up between my legs. I blushed.

"Thank you."

"You don't need to thank me, Pres." I sat up and Xavier passed me my shorts. "Are you going to stay tonight?" I shook my head. He reached over and untied the silk tie from my neck.

"I shouldn't. Eve is going to have my head in the morning and if she sees me missing-"

"If she's being this horrible to you then I'll speak to her."

"No, it's okay. I got this." I stood up and slipped my shorts back on. Xavier grabbed me by the hips and pulled me against him. I wrapped my arms around his neck and stepped on to my tip toes so that we were almost the same height.

"When everyone goes out for dinner tomorrow. I want to take you out. Then you could join them later on. I'll even come out too." He tucked hair behind my ear.

"Yeah, I'd like that." I pressed a light kiss on his lips. I removed my arms and stepped back. "I'm gonna sneak back down, I'll bring your coffee in the morning."

"Sweet dreams."

"And you." I walked over to the door and grabbed the door handle. I chewed on my lip and turned back around. "I'm texting Killian. And I like him." Xavier crossed his arms.

"I know."

"And I like you."

"And I you. No one is asking you to choose, only you're thinking that. I mentioned him because I want you to normalise it in your head."

"Okay. Thank you, Captain." I forced and smiled then crept out of his cabin, sneaking back to my own.

chapter thirteen

Xavier had given me some things to think about and I spent an hour before I fell back to sleep trying to type a text to Killian. In the end I didn't think it was the best idea to try and explain things in a text message. Not something like that.

I was exhausted when I woke up. My lack of sleep was beginning to wear me down, but I was thankful it was a drop off day, and I hadn't had to be a part of breakfast service thanks to Xavier's orders. That was down to Eve.

However as soon as I heard the conversations inside the crew mess I wanted to crawl right back into my cabin.

"So I was on anchor watch last night and I swear that I heard Captain banging someone. Think Eve finally got her claws into Capt?" The thought of Eve going anywhere near

Xavier made me sick to my stomach, the only thing that made me feel better was the fact I knew it was me inside his cabin. Apparently not even a gag would work on me.

I knew I couldn't risk messing around with him while people were on the bridge again. I was going to get caught and then it would cause more drama than it was worth. Though I wasn't sure of that statement. While my feelings were growing for the man on the other side of the phone, they were also growing for my Captain.

The words that Xavier had said to me last night, that liking both of them weren't a problem, that I shouldn't think of it that way, were rattling around in my head.

I walked into the crew mess. Ben and Elliot were sitting down eating breakfast and gossiping.

"Oh hey, Pres." Ben spoke with a mouthful of rice krispies.

"Good morning, Pres." Elliot smiled.

"Morning guys."

"Cap had someone in his cabin last night. I heard them." Ben spoke.

"Wow, right, okay." I answered. The shock on my face wasn't fake, I couldn't quite get over the fact how blunt he had been.

"It was either Eve or a hooker. I'm saying it was Eve."

"Nah, hooker. So easy to sneak onto the boat."

"Just because you think that Cap was shagging someone doesn't mean that he paid for it." May strolled down to the crew mess, walking over to the spare radio batteries and swapping hers out.

"To be fair, Cap is pretty hot." Elliot shrugged.

"Agreed, we're lucky Killian wanted to give his best friend a boat to run." May shrugged, running back upstairs.

"Well you guys have fun, I'm gonna go make Captain's coffee." I told them.

"You're not having breakfast?" Ben asked.

"Nah, bit of an upset stomach. See you guys later." I grabbed my radio from the charger station and hooked it onto my skirt. I walked up the stairs, putting my ear piece in. Jameson was clearing from breakfast and the oven was most likely prepping crew lunch.

"Morning, James." I smiled, walking over to the stew pantry.

"Hey girlie." He glanced over his shoulder. "Are Ben and Elliot still gossiping about Cap?" He asked. I hummed. A silence settled over us and it wasn't long until I felt eyes burning into my skull while I made Xaviers coffee. "Pres, why on earth are you being so quiet..." He trailed off. I looked over at him and jumped back when I realised how close he was to me.

"Just trying not to burn my hands with boiling water."

"I've known you less than a month and I can tell when you are lying." He raised a brow at me. I looked away and stared down into the frothy coffee mug. "Oh please tell me you did..." I glanced at him in the corner of my eye and gave a slight nod, that was enough to have Jameson's arms wrapped around me. Not the reaction I was expecting. "Oh my fucking god, you got in there girl. I'm jealous, tell me, is he as big as I think he is?"

"Shh, can we just keep it quiet?" I asked pulling away.

"Yeah, of course. Me and you are gonna talk later. I need every little detail." Jameson kissed the top of my head and I laughed.

I stopped being nervous when I went to give Xavier his morning coffee, it was something that I looked forward to, something that would get me through the day with the she-devil. I walked through the door and into the bridge. Xavier was sitting in his little seating area, reading through some paperwork with his glasses on again.

"Morning." I announced. Xavier looked up at me and my heart clenched as he smiled. I placed his coffee down on the table and scouted the area outside for the deck crew, then placed my hands on the table and leant over to give him a quick kiss. Our lips barely touched and it killed me inside.

"Morning, my sweet girl. How are you feeling?" I stepped back and placed my hands behind my back.

"Looking forward to dropping off. And relaxing."

"We have a couple of days til our next charter so I'm giving everyone the rest of the day off. You still look dead on your feet." He lifted his coffee to his lips.

"You don't have to do that because of me."

"And if I don't then Eve is just going to keep pushing you."

"It's not your fault." I shrugged.

"I'm not stupid, Presley. I know why Eve acts the way she does. And in this case she wouldn't be wrong."

"But she doesn't know, so it's okay. She'll give in eventually." I didn't know if I should have told him about what everyone was saying in the crew mess, or the fact that James had taken one look at me and knew I was the girl.

"I'll talk to Killian."

"There's no need honestly, Eve has been around for a long time and if she wants to keep pretending that she has you then let her. Everyone knows that it's not true."

"As long as you do that's all that matters." He reached over to let his fingertips brush my cheeks, leaving them blushed where he had touched them.

"I'll see you later." I told him.

"I'm looking forward to our dinner."

"Me too."

No matter if you love your job or not, there is always a part of you that looks forward to the end of your day or the end of your shift. We all looked forward to charter guests leaving, and even with flipping over the boat it was bliss.

"I'd just like to say thank you for all your hard work." The primary spoke, placing her hands on her heart, and acting like she was touched. "Although there were a few things that everyone could improve on. Service wasn't as fast as we would have liked, at times there was only one person to tend to us, which I think for the amount of money I paid to be here, isn't right."

There were also moments when you wanted to scream out loud. Her every wish was tended to and she was waited on hand and foot. I glanced over to my right and spotted

Chessa slightly shaking her head, which told me even she agreed that our service couldn't have been any better.

"Anyway, thank you, have a nice season. And work on your service for your next guests." The primary handed over a stack of cash to Captain Xavier but there was no way we could figure out how much it was with how it had been folded.

"Thank you." Captain Xavier nodded at her. The bitch walked off the boat and when they were an ear shot away Jameson opened his mouth.

"What a bunch of bitches." He scoffed.

"Agreed, they were beyond awful." Chessa spoke up. Eve looked down the line, right at me.

"Maybe there could be some improvements in speed." She raised her brow at me.

"I don't know Eve, Presley was like a whippet out there the other night. Two martinis in under a minute." Chessa backed me up. I gave her a small smile to say thank you.

"And from what I saw last night Eve, Presley was left on her own." Xavier glared at her. Eve looked like a deer caught in headlights being called out by the Captain. "I sent Presley to bed last night because she hadn't had a break and you had gone down. No one was there to help her and Chessa didn't know she needed any help because Presley wanted to prove to you that she is good at what she does."

"Cap-" She started.

"I'll deal with you later. You have the rest of the day off, the boat can be flipped tomorrow." Xavier walked off.

There was an awkward silence on deck and I chewed on my lip. Everyone was giving glances at one another, mostly towards Eve.

"He had a point, Eve. I didn't even know she was on her own." I did a double take. The last thing I expected was for Chessa to speak up against her best friend and Chief Stew.

"Oh right, so I'm the bad guy?" She exclaimed and stormed off.

"Yeah you are, bitch." May mumbled under her breath on the other side of me. "Come on, let's all get wasted!" May grabbed my hand and pulled me into the boat.

chapter fourteen

May didn't like the fact I told her I wanted to stay behind for dinner because I wanted to call home. I felt awful for lying to her, but my heart beat over time when I thought about getting to have dinner with Xavier. By the time it hit five everyone was off the boat and I threw my blanket off my body and rushed to get ready.

My eyeliner failed multiple times before I managed to get it right because I was shaking that much. I took longer with my make up, taking time to give myself some extra glam and hide the bags under my eyes. I decided on wearing a silk red cowl dress that tied behind the curve against my hips. I paired it with a pair of nude wedge heels that complemented the tan I was beginning to build on my legs.

I grabbed my clutch and walked up into the galley, to make my way to the bridge. I walked through the lounge and went to head upstairs but a new voice caught my attention, a familiar one.

"Presley?" I turned around to be faced with a smartly dressed Killian, a pair of black trousers and a black shirt. His shoes were freshly polished and his hair was newly trimmed. He looked gorgeous and I couldn't take my eyes away from him, my shock adding to the pressure.

I was dressed and ready to get my socks blown off by Xavier and now Killian was here. I'd thought a lot about what Xavier had said to me, that I'd be surprised by Killian but it didn't stop the guilt flowing through my body when I looked him in the eye.

"Killian-"

"Come talk on the sundeck with me." He held out his hand. My eyes flickered towards the stairs that led to Xavier and back at Killian who was waiting patiently for me.

"Okay." I answered and walked towards him. Killian interlinked our hands and I smiled as I looked down on them. It felt right, and I felt safe with him. I knew I needed to talk to Killian, it was easy to avoid something through a text message. I also didn't know that Killian was coming back, he hadn't said anything.

Killian guided me to the sun deck, pulling me gently behind him. We stopped, standing on the port side overlooking the anchorage and out to sea.

"I didn't know you were coming back." I put a hand on the rails and bit my lip. Killian leaned against them, arms folded over his chest.

"I missed you, you know that." He smiled at me. I nodded and stared out at the water.

"I missed you too."

"So why are you all dressed up on an empty boat?" He asked. There was a moment of silence between us before I answered.

"A couple of things happened while you were away...just don't get mad I guess?" Killian and I weren't official but that didn't mean I wanted to hurt his feelings. I was stuck between two best friends and despite what Xavier had told me, I was nervous. Killian watched me, waiting for me to carry on. "The past couple of weeks, Xavier and I...have been sleeping together."

I waited for the bomb to drop, and when it did it wasn't what I expected. Killian pulled me against him, his hands on my waist, and a deep kiss placed on my lips. Out of instinct I wrapped my arms around his neck and pulled him closer against me. I'd missed the taste of spearmint on his breath and the way his kisses consumed me, making my brain stop working. All sense was thrown out of the window when it came to either of them.

There was a chuckle from behind us and I jumped back, putting as much space as I could between Killian and I. My stomach churned at the sight of Xavier standing behind us. I didn't dare open my mouth to speak in fear that I puke the contents of my stomach up.

"You bastard." Killian shook his head.

"I couldn't help it, it was like the perfect ending of those movies your little sister loves with the background behind you." Xavier teased. Watching the scene unfold in front of me made my head spin a thousand miles an hour.

I felt as if some big game had been played on me. That they were both in on it.

"Presley. Are you okay?" Killian furrowed his brows at me.

"I feel sick." I whispered.

"Sweet girl, come here." Xavier walked towards me and when he got close I took a step backwards.

"Love, what's wrong?" Killian stood straight, the concern growing further on his face.

"This has just been one big game to you, both of you." Tears rolled down my face and the two men looked at one another as my breathing was fast and uneven. Panic setting in.

"Not at all." Killian shook his head.

"You know where I stand on this, Presley." Xavier's face was soft and he looked almost hurt that I could suggest something like that. "I told you that I didn't care if you had been with Killian."

"And I don't care about Xavier, love. I honestly don't care. We both care about you."

"You laughed." I gulped.

"I laughed for the reason I told Killian. I meant nothing of it, my sweet girl." Killian took the opportunity to pull me against him. My body relaxed against him but my eyes were on Xavier.

"Do you want to know my dream?" Killian whispered against my hair. "It's you. And me. And Xavier. Together. This isn't a game." My eyes were locked onto Xavier's and slowly he reached us, putting out his hand to stroke my cheek.

"Why?"

"Because that's what we want. Can't that just be enough?" Xavier answered. "Let's go to dinner like we planned and we can talk about it, the three of us. Just please don't run from it." I nodded, and Killian loosened his grip on me.

"Do you want to go check your make up?" I touched my cheeks, feeling the dampness from my tears. I shook my head.

"I have powder in my bag." I spoke quietly, looking between both of the men.

"Come on then let's go sort this out." Xavier held out his hand to me and I stepped out of Killian's arms to take it.

Once we had walked off the boat, Killian took my other hand and I was sandwiched between the two gorgeous men as we walked off the dock. My eyes were darting anywhere, looking out for the rest of the crew in case they were heading back to the boat. At the end of the dock there was a small car park for a few cars and taxis.

Killian pulled a set of car keys out of his pocket and pressed the button. A car on the edge of the car park lit up, a matte black Mercedes Benz. A small smile danced on my lips because Killian was the definition of a typical rich man and yet somehow had his soul. Killian let go of my hand

and Xavier twirled me around, making me laugh. Killian had opened the passenger door for me and I slipped down into the low seat, trying to tug down my dress so I didn't flash my underwear. I reached for my belt but Killian got there before me, reaching over to buckle me in. A quick kiss on my lips before he stood and shut the car door.

Xavier climbed in the back seat behind Killian, despite having less room, but his gaze was trained on me and I suspected that was why he had done it. Killian climbed into the car and started the engine.

"Did you book the usual restaurant we go to?" Killian asked his best friend.

"Called ahead when you got here, knew you'd gate crash." Xavier smirked as Killian pulled out of the car park.

My body finally relaxed in the car as we drove down the Italian streets, watching the world pass by through the window. The sky was almost dark and the street lights were left to light up the city. We weren't in the car for long and there wasn't any sort of awkward silence in the car. The silence was safe and comfortable, everyone was happily left with their own thoughts.

It took me a moment to think about what I was doing, I was playing with fire. Two men wanted me, wanted to share me and I wasn't saying no. For once in my life I was doing what I wanted and I didn't want to have to pick between either of them.

Killian stopped the car outside a restaurant in the middle of the town. Xavier slipped out the car first and I unhooked my seat belt as he opened the door for me. I took his hand to help balance myself on the uneven path. Killian stepped out of the car and handed his keys to the valet that was waiting by the side of the car. The valet climbed into the car and carefully drove off.

The restaurant was beautiful and lit up the entire street. There was seating lining the outside of the restaurant, couples having dinner together, loved up. Inside I could see groups of friends laughing together.

The two men stood either side of me, each offering their arms. For a moment I had to think about who to choose, then it crossed my mind that the entire point of this dinner was to talk about the possibility of being with them both. Somehow we managed to fit through the double door and stand in front of the host.

It was a middle aged man with a salt and pepper beard, dressed in a suit and tie. I expected us to be given weird looks considering I was hanging off the arms of two men like a hooker. Only instead he smiled and greeted them both by name. The host collected three menus, putting them under his arm.

"This way, we have your table on the terrace." He spoke with a thick Italian accent.

"Thank you, Frank."

I followed the Host upstairs to a small dining area that led to a beautiful terrace that overlooked the city. Trellis either side of the balcony to give protection to customers from the wind. Flowers and vine curling around it and across the railing. It was beautiful, beyond beautiful.

The Host put out his hand towards a square table in the corner with three chairs pushed against the balcony. Xavier took a step forward and pulled out the chair that would place me in the middle of them. I held down my dress and slid into the seat thanking Xavier. He pushed me in like a gentleman and sat down. Killian took the other seat, glancing at me to smile. The Host put down the three menus in front of us.

"Can I get you anything to drink before you order?"

"Bottle of your expensive champagne." Killian answered.

"Of course, Sir." The Host scurried off leaving the three of us alone. There was a candle lit in the middle of the table, set on an ivory table cloth.

"Always spending the cash aren't we, friend?" Xavier teased.

"What else do I need it for if not to treat people who I care about." That included me. My cheeks blushed and I smiled at him.

"That guy, he didn't look at us strangely, like this was normal for the two of you." Killian and Xavier looked at one another, a silent conversation between the two of them.

"Xav and I have…shared girlfriends before." I leant back in my chair, blinking in shock. "Except it's never worked out. Not for long."

"The women we've been with always end up wanting one of us and trying to play us against one another."

"And up until you, love, we had given up."

"What on earth made you think I'd be up for being with you both?" I folded my arms. I mean it was one hell of an assumption, and the fact that they had both planned to sleep with me and not even tell me. I was slightly pissed off.

"Honestly from the moment I saw you humming to yourself in my cabin." Killian smiled at me.

"You walked onto the bridge and your eyes were lit up, like this was the most exciting thing. Full of life." Xavier added.

"We didn't have to propose the idea to you. You liked us both on your own accord."

"Did you know that I'd slept with Xavier?" I asked.

"No. Not until you told me. But I knew that he'd heard that pretty little mouth of yours." He reached out, brushing a finger over my lips and I blushed, finding myself a little less pissed at him. "So I had suspicions."

"You're both unbelievable." Before I could rant my head off, Frank, the Host, returned with the bottle of Champagne and juggling three glasses in one hand. He placed a glass in front of each of us, and poured the bubbly. It was nice to be served instead of serving.

"Do you need a few more moments to look at the menu?" Frank nodded towards our menus that hadn't moved an inch. I blushed and turned my head, Frank knew that they'd shared girlfriends before so he knew exactly why I was there. Except I wasn't theirs, and I hadn't decided if I wanted to be yet.

"Please, Frank."

I picked up my menu and started to look over what they had, and not carry on the conversation. Those few moments of silence gave me enough time to process the first parts of the information that I had been given. There had been girls before me, and when I thought of that I found myself jealous. I questioned if that also made me greedy, wanting both of them. While Xavier had told me it was okay to want both of them, at that point I was already starting to develop feelings for them both. I just hadn't considered that I hadn't needed to pick and my heart should have been full of relief that I didn't have to.

Frank returned a few minutes later and asked me what I'd like to order first,

"Carbonara please, with fries." Frank turned to Killian.

"Fillet steak, please." Then to Xavier.

"Same as the lady." He answered and closed his menu. Frank collected the three menus and left the table.

"The first time I came to Italy when I was younger, my mom bullied me for ordering fries." I smiled, breaking the silence between us.

"I find it's a stupid tourist thing to say, most people think just because you're in another country you can't eat the things you usually love."

The rest of dinner was small talk and taking the opportunity to learn more about one another. I found myself completely unwinding from the stress of the charter and laughing at the jokes that the two men made. During our conversations Killian reached out and took my hand in his, and Xavier placed his hand on my knee.

Killian and Xavier split the bill between them and we left the restaurant. The three of us collected Killian's car and we drove back to the harbour. Xavier helped me out of the car and the three of us stood overlooking the dock full of extremely expensive boats. At least they were to me, they were probably pennies to Killian.

"Have you thought about what I asked you?" Killian nudged me. I looked up at him.

"A little." I answered.

"What did he ask you?" Xavier questioned, leaning over the railings further.

"He asked me what my dream in life was, where I want to be in life."

"So what's your answer?" Killian spoke.

"I don't want to go back to London, I know that. I think I'm falling in love with Italy. And I want to do a few seasons on yachts, save and put a deposit on my own little hotel." I explained. "Just something small and mine." I glanced at Killian and Xavier, who were looking at me in awe. I blushed, chewing on my lip. "And I think I have room for a couple of guys in my life."

"Really?" Killian smirked.

"I'm willing to give it a try, I don't know how it works but I want to try, because I've somehow caught feelings for both of you and I don't want to choose."

Killian grabbed my face and kissed me with so much force that I was taken back, losing all the oxygen that was in my lungs as he claimed me. I was pulled away by my waist and Xavier took control. His lips pressed against mine like waves crashing against the shore. It didn't feel as if my kiss with Killian had been cut short, my heart raced at being passed between them. When Xavier pulled away and brushed my hair away from my face I stared at him dazed.

A hand snaked around my waist from behind, Killian was inches away from the sensitive area between my legs. I settled against him, while Xavier dipped down to kiss my neck. From two small but steamy kisses, there was no doubt that together these men would ruin me.

I had to come to my senses and not allow myself to be dragged back to the boat for the rest of the night. I'd promised May that I'd join them later on and despite my new dating situation, I couldn't let down one of my closest friends.

"Stop." I whispered. I cleared my throat. "We can't. I promised May I would join her and the rest of the crew." Xavier pulled away from leaving soft kisses on my neck. "You can both come, the crew would love that, and then later on we can get back to this." I spewed out before I changed my mind.

Killian chuckled.

"Are you sure about that love?"

"Yes." I pulled myself out of his grasp, and put a metre distance between the two of them, so my brain wasn't overloaded by the things that could happen. "Come on, let's go." I ordered and started to walk off towards the end of the seafront strip, where the few clubs the crew always ended up at were.

I looked over my shoulder, both men happily following me in stride with one another and smiles on their faces. Which left a smile on mine.

chapter fifteen

I DIDN'T NEED TO look for May because a few steps into the club and I was rammed into her body as she came flying from the crowd. Her arms wrapped around my neck tightly, suffocating me. When she finally pulled away she grabbed my face and kissed my cheek, completely and utterly wasted already.

"I was starting to give up on you." She shouted over the music.

"I promised, didn't I? I think I have some catching up to do though by the state of you." I laughed.

"For that you're necking down tequila, sweetie." She wagged her finger at me.

"Hello May." Killian appeared by my side with Xavier standing beside him.

"Oh my god, you both came too! Shots time!" She screamed at the top of her voice, grabbing my hand and pulling me towards the bar.

May didn't stop at ordering me one shot, she ordered three each, determined to make sure that I caught up with her and the rest of the crew before dragging us over to the booth that they had reserved. There was enough space for all of us, although Eve didn't want to budge up when she saw me. She was soon on her feet when she saw Xavier step up behind me. He kept his distance from me, but I could still feel his lips on mine as Eve stood up to greet him and brown nose him, all in hopes that he would fall madly in love with her.

It was cruel of me to laugh at her, even if it was inside, and even though she had tried at every point to make work a living hell just because she wanted Xavier.

Getting drunk was exactly what I needed, dancing under the hot lights, twirling and giggly with May. We dragged James onto the floor with us, with protest. I had two watchers from the side of the room. Both of their eyes sneakily on me and as the night went on, I was hot and flushed with a need to know exactly what it was like to have them at once. The alcohol was definitely clouding my judgement.

I couldn't let on what my mind was saying because if the crew found out then all hell would break loose.

I threw myself down on the booth sofa, leaning back onto Ben who was betting with Phoenix if Elliot would get the number of the girl he was chatting up. They were like a bunch of tight knit brothers, I was beginning to understand that the whole boat worked as a family. It made me question the reactions I would get if anyone else found out about Killian, Xavier and I. I wondered if they even knew that the men liked to share a girlfriend between them, because it had been a shock to me.

"Hello, earth to Presley?" Ben waved his hand in my face and I blinked, snapping out of my spiralling drunk thoughts.

"I'm craving a greasy kebab." I told him. Ben laughed at me.

"That's so British of you. The only place I can think of that's even open is a hole in the wall pizza place. Pizza the size of your head."

"Yes." I sat up, grabbing his face and pressed a big kiss on his forehead. "Pizza. Let's go."

"Well I suppose I win if we have to pull Elliot away early." Phoenix spoke up, putting his arm around Ben's shoulder.

Phoenix slipped under the table in his drunk state and I laughed at him. Our bosun gathered the rest of the crew around the booth, except Elliot who was still flirting. Xavier and Killian stood at the steps of the booth, Killian casually leaning against the railing, and Xavier stood with his arms folded.

"I declare Pizza!" Phoenix shouted and cheered.

"Not having to cook for you drunk lot, happy days." Jameson scoffed.

After dragging Elliot away from the new love of his life, all of them walked in a zig zagged mess up the street to the small pizza place that Ben had mentioned.

It was a small hole in the wall, with a narrow pizza kitchen next to a gelato store that was closed for the night. In the shop window there were slices of pizza that could have counted as a whole pizza themselves. Killian being the generous boss he was, paid for them all tapping his card like it was nothing. We all laughed and giggled on our way back to the dock, I was starting to sober up and my heels were beginning to hurt but laughing with May and Jameson, linking arms while still trying to eat made me forget again. It was one of the happiest moments of my life,

I felt free and settled even if I was living in an extremely small cabin.

I looked over my shoulder, catching a glance of the two men that had taken me to dinner, my heart pounding faster when Killian smirked at me. His eyes took a glance at my ass in my dress. I quickly whipped my head around before my blush gave me away.

"I'm so glad we have a couple of days off." May sighed. "Oh shit." She turned around and directed her attention to Killian. "Are you staying, boss? Are we on the clock?"

"You're off the clock, May. I'm just here to see your Captain." He chuckled.

"Thank god." She mumbled. "Ooo I might book a hotel room tomorrow. Big double bed and a big round bath with jets." She moaned, taking a bite from her pizza.

The rest of the walk down the dock May spoke about how she was going to enjoy stretching her legs in bed, even when Xavier reminded her that she needed to ask permission to leave the boat. When we got to the boat, the deck team and James decided that they were going to raid the freezer for ice cream, leaving the interior crew in the main lounge.

Eve was sitting on the sofa, her skirt raised a little two high as she sipped on a vodka tonic she had made for herself. Her eyes were completely trained on Xavier. I couldn't stick around and watch, carefully and quietly I slipped out. I hoped that if everyone was doing their own thing after their hangovers, that I would manage to get some more time with Killian and Xavier.

I walked into the galley where the deck crew were sitting on the floor eating ice cream from the tub and sat down beside May, stealing her spoon for a mouthful myself.

"Hey girlie." She mumbled, leaning her head on me. Despite not spending much time with the deck crew other than May, they were a lot more welcoming than the interior crew. While I sat there sobering up, I listened to them bicker about who was cleaning the stainless steel rails tomorrow.

"I'm going to bed." I whispered to May. She nodded at me and kissed my cheek. "Night love ya."

"Love you too."

I lay in bed, listening to the sound of them in the galley and scrolling through Instagram. It wasn't long after that May stumbled into her bunk and fell asleep. The room filled with her snores again. The moment I put my phone down a text message came through.

'Xav's cabin. Now.'

I peaked under my bunk to check that May was asleep before climbing down and sneaking out, which had become a regular occurrence. I couldn't hear anyone else awake and quickly navigated myself through the dark, my heart was beating out of my chest. Killian's message had sounded less than impressed and I thought that they had changed their mind about wanting to try things with the three of us.

I knocked quietly on the cabin door and whipped my head left and right to check for anyone. Xavier opened the door, standing in his pyjama bottoms, his hair pushed back with a headband. I slipped inside the room, chewing on my lip and before I could open my mouth, I had Killian's hand around my throat and pinning me to the door.

"We have unfinished business, love. Who said you get to sleep tonight?"

chapter sixteen

"You were busy." I whispered.

"Like either of us wanted to spend more time with Eve than we have to. We were only there to be polite to Chessa." Xavier scoffed, taking his seat at his desk.

"I've heard about how good those lips of yours are at sucking cock, I think it's my turn don't you?" Killian smirked. "Are you going to suck my cock while Xavier watches, my love?" I did my best attempt to nod, Killian released me and his hands reached for the silky button up shirt I was wearing. He tore the top open with his hands and I gasped. A few buttons bounced across the room as the cold sea air perked my nipples.

My eyes glanced over at Xavier, who sat on his leather desk chair, legs wide open palming himself as he stared at me. The tent under his bottoms growing with every second.

"We're both going to take you tonight you know that don't you?" Killian whispered in my ear. "How many times have you thought about it, my filthy stew?"

"Daily." I sassed back trying to gain some control, although there wasn't much point.

Killian unbuttoned his shirt, threw it to the ground, and took off his trousers. He had no shame of being stark naked in front of his best friend, and I had to remind myself they had done this before. He sat against the pillows on Xavier's bed and motioned for me to come to him. I pushed down my shorts, and crawled my way up the bed, coming face to face with his hard cock. I kept eye contact with Killian as I teased the tip of him with light kisses. The frustration grew on his face and as I slipped the head into my mouth I looked at Xavier who had pulled his own hard cock out from his bottoms and used his hand.

I closed my eyes, taking more of Killian into my mouth and what I couldn't fit in there I used one of my hands. I hollowed my cheeks and created more suction, hitting the right spot that had Killian hissing and taking a fist full of my hair.

"Fucking hell, she's good." Killian hissed.

"I told you, she's fucking perfect." Xavier replied. I swirled my tongue just under the head that caused Killian to jolt. I could taste the pre-cum leaking from him and I forced him further down my throat, testing my limits as I gagged on him. Killian moaned, his grip on my hair loosened for a moment, as he lost his senses.

I bobbed my head harder and faster on his cock, having some control of Killian made me feel a lot more confident than last time. I could feel Xavier's eyes on me, watching my lips around Killian's cock. I glanced to the side still moving my head, Killian's hand tugging on my hair. His eyes glazed over and I had the feeling he was struggling to hold back. I looked up at Killian whose eyes were rolling into the back of his head.

I didn't hear Xavier stand up and position himself behind me. Killian's lips turned up into a smirk and I pulled away from his cock. My lips going numb before I could talk, Xavier buried himself inside of me. I gasped at Xavier's cock stretching me out, his hands resting on my hips. Slowly he pulled out and then pulled my hips back down onto his cock.

"You okay there, my sweet girl?" Xavier teased. "I don't think either of us told you to stop." Xavier's hand made contact with my ass cheek and I moaned at the sharp sting on my skin.

"Suck." Killian lifted my head up so I'd look at him, as Xavier slowly thrusted inside of me. I lowered my head again, holding his cock in my hand and took my time as I got used to Xavier being inside of me.

I carried on sucking Killian's cock who loved to lay back and be worshipped, despite the show he had put on worshipping me on the sky deck. I was beginning to think maybe it was our thing, worshipping and building one another up. While Xavier took care of me, made sure I slept enough or at least got rest.

I put all of my concentration into taking as much of Killian inside of my mouth as I could while ignoring the fact that Xavier was fucking me from behind. Killian pushed my head further onto him making me choke and he moaned loudly. I pulled up, using my tongue and taking a moment to breathe while the heat built inside of my stomach. Xavier started to thrust harder into me, Killian's fingers found their way to my clit and I pulled my mouth off again, almost toppling over the edge. My breath hitched and squeezed my eyes shut.

Killian's fingers moved faster against my clit in rhythm to Xavier's thrusts. I hid my face in Killian's thigh, as Xavier thrusted into me with one sharp thrust, sending me over the edge and cumming over his cock. Except Xavier hadn't come and I realised it was only the beginning, and I'd be cumming again before the night was over. Just cumming once had completely sobered me up, and my nerves were flooding through about what would happen next. Xavier pulled out of me, and lifted me up into his arms, placing a sweet kiss on my lips. Killian moved further down the bed and Xavier passed me into his arms instead.

I was straddling Killian this time, my wet pussy over the top of his hard cock. Xavier took his position again behind me.

"What are we doing?" I asked, looking over and up over my shoulder at him.

"Remember when I stretched that tight little pussy of yours with my fist. Have you maybe thought there was a reason for that?" He raised his eyebrow at me.

"Two partners, love." I looked down at Killian. "Meaning there's two cocks to fill you up."

"I think this is the time I should be telling you to stick it in my ass instead, but even that sounds terrifying."

"There will be plenty of time for that, don't worry." Killian cupped the back of my neck and pulled me down for a kiss, giving him the right position to slip inside of me. I put my hands either side of his head and kissed him back with as much force as I could. I pulled away when I felt the cold wet fingers alongside Killian's cock.

"We need to make sure that you don't get hurt." Xavier spoke. "Relax, we'll take care of you."

"Are you sure?" I asked.

"We've got you." Killian kissed me gently again, distracting me. Slowly, Killian began to move and carefully Xavier pushed his fingers in further, stretching me out, and when he finally managed to push three in alongside Killian's cock he praised me.

"Good girl, that's our good girl. She's going to take us so well Kil." I closed my eyes, allowing myself to work with the pleasure I was feeling against the sting of being stretched. Killian soothed me as Xavier worked his fingers to make enough room for him to fit alongside Killian. The more I thought about it, the more the knot in my stomach twisted my insides. The thought of being stretched out by the two men who wanted to share me made me clench around their cock and fingers cumming again.

"Well done, love. Every time you cum the more your body relaxes for us."

Xavier pulled out his fingers and I was aware of the sound of the bottle cap being flipped open. Killian stopped moving.

"Why'd you stop?" I questioned.

"Just breathe for me, love." He answered, moving one hand towards my clit and slowly tracing circles to help my pussy relax.

I felt Xavier push his cock at my already stuffed pussy and I was afraid that between them they would tear me apart, until he pushed the head of his cock inside of me. I hissed and bared the slight pain of being stretched so far, thinking back to the night Xavier had pushed his entire fist inside of me.

"Are you okay?" Xavier asked.

"More." I whispered. He pushed further inside me, the fullness causing my pussy to throb and wonder what it was going to feel like once he was fully inside of me. There were small beads of sweat on my forehead that Killian wiped away from underneath me.

I moaned once I knew he was as deep inside me as possible, and my mind was fogged with thoughts of how much I wanted to be fucked. My men picked it up and began to move in sync together, pulling in and out, their dicks rubbing together as they stuffed my pussy full. I hid myself against Killian, arching my back further for better access. Killian and Xavier worked together as a team that had me covering my moans with the sheets and gripping them so tightly I thought my nails were going through them.

They both began to thrust into me faster, the pain was completely gone and I was only left with the pleasure. They moved easily inside of me and I could feel the walls inside of my pussy tightening again. Third time round I was beginning to lose control of myself and all I happily felt like was a slut who was getting the best fuck of her life.

"Need, to, cum." I mumbled, loud enough that Killian could hear me over the sounds of thrusting.

"I'm close too." He kissed the side of my head. "Xav?"

"Fuck, on three. One, two, three."

I had never been filled with so much cum in my life. I could feel it leaking from the sides while I was still stretched around two cocks. Xavier was the first to pull out and I slumped against Killian, who rolled us over and then pulled his softening cock out as well. I lay there starry eyed and completely spent. Killian reached down between my legs and I whined, already feeling the after effects of being stretched out. He used two fingers to scoop out the mixture of cum and brought them to my lips. I wrapped my mouth around his fingers, swallowing the cum from them. It tasted sweet.

"You're ours now, Presley." He leant down and pecked my lips once I was done. I hummed in response. Xavier sat beside me on the bed and I turned to face him. He reached out to stroke my hair.

"Stay with us tonight, please?" I was too tired to even consider moving.

"Can someone clean me up?" I mumbled. "I'm so so tired." My eyes closed gently. I heard one of them say yes, but it could have also been both of them. The last thing I remembered was being tucked in between the two men who were well on their way to stealing my heart.

chapter seventeen

THERE WAS NO ALARM set, so when I finally woke up it was with a jolt. I sat up in bed startled and hot from being wedged between Xavier and Killian. My abrupt wake up disturbed them too. Killian groaned and rolled over towards me and Xavier carefully sat up.

"Where's the fire?" He yawned.

"What time is it? Someone might know I'm gone." I leaned over him and looked at the small clock on his bedside table. It was nine and I was completely fucked. I climbed out the bottom of the bed as Killian woke up too. I helped myself to clothes of Xavier's and hoped that no one would be able to smell him on me. If I was wearing a t-shirt and joggers at least I could style out that I'd been for a walk.

The ache between my legs was intense and I hoped that I could still walk normally without questions about who had railed me into next week by May.

"Kiss before you leave us." Killian ordered, his eyes still half shut. I rushed back over quickly giving each man a kiss that lasted no longer than a second before rushing out of the cabin.

It made it easier that everyone was asleep still when I snuck back down. How no one had ever caught me was beyond me. I was the luckiest bitch alive.

I held my breath as I slipped inside May and I's cabin. I slipped inside and carefully closed the door. I navigated myself in the dark back to the safety of my bunk. It was anything but safe as my phone lit up with a new message. Confusion drowned me as I looked at a video attachment. I made sure the volume was down on my phone before opening the attachment.

It was dark at first. The camera moved around quickly and blurred, then it focused on a small slip between a door and the frame. A perfect view of my body being used by the two men who I'd spent the night with. My blood ran cold but my ears were on fire as I stared at the video that was almost two minutes long. One of the crew had been up, they caught us on camera and no doubt they wanted to make my life a living hell now that they knew.

Everything I had wanted to avoid had come true in a split second. There was no way I was going to get any more sleep. My phone screen was imprinted into my head.

May woke up an hour later and I found myself glancing at her as she got ready for the day. I questioned if it could be her, but May was one of my closest friends.

I got myself ready for the day, completely exhausted and my head pounding. The rest of my body was just as broken from Killian and Xavier.

I kept my head down as I restocked the fridges on the sky deck, wanting to avoid everyone as I sorted out my head.

The sound of footsteps disturbed my peace and I lifted my head over the bar to see Eve walking towards me. I don't suppose it was really much of a surprise to see the smirk on her face. I sighed and mumbled to myself of course it had been her. She had been after Xavier for years and she hated my guts for it since I stepped on board.

The look on her face said it all. A cross between a smirk and the look that she wanted to murder me. I attempted to ignore her as I carried on with my jobs but I could feel her eyes burning into the back of my skull.

"Imagine what everyone else would say if they knew you were a dirty little whore." She finally spoke. I stood up for the confrontation knowing that it wasn't going to end well. My heart was already beating out of my chest and I could barely hear the sea over the sound of it in my ears.

"It's none of your business." I spoke, my voice cracking at the end. "What you did was illegal and you're lucky if I don't call the police."

"Call them see if I care," Eve stepped into my personal space, we were almost touching. "What I suggest is you pack your bags and get the first flight back to London. The Yachting world is a small one and I'd hate for your Auntie's reputation to be ruined because her niece is a little slut." She snarled.

"Why? Why do this? Do you really want the Captain that badly?"

"I've been here for five years and you waltz in like you're perfect and manage to take him from me, and Killian?"

"He wasn't yours in the first place." I whispered.

The fuse in Eva sparked and before I knew it she shoved me to the deck like we were children on the playground.

"Leave. I'll show the whole crew in six hours if you're not gone. And if you even think about telling Captain or Killian,

I'll throw you overboard." Eve turned on her heel, strutted off.

I pulled my legs up to my body and took a deep breath as the pain on my ass settled. Tears were flowing freely from my eyes and I could barely function. She'd show the whole crew, and tell the whole community and my Aunt would truly kill me for breaking the number one rule.

I wiped the tears from under my eyes and stood up from the deck. I grabbed the empty boxes from filling the fridge and walked down to the main deck. I managed to hide my face as I dodged the deck crew cleaning the stainless and into the main salon.

Getting through the galley was the hard part, Jameson saw me coming though and managed to grab my arm before I could get into the crew mess.

"Hey what's just happened?" He asked, looking over the crying mess of my face. I tried to open my mouth but nothing came out. "Shit, Pres." He pulled me into the kitchen area and grabbed a fresh towel to dab my tears away. "Come on, tell me what happened." He spoke softly. I swallowed and took a deep breath.

"Eve has a video of me." I croaked. "Of me, in bed, with Captain, and with Killian." Jameson's face dropped and it took him a moment to process what I was telling him. "Did you just say Killian? As in you were sleeping with them both? Together?" I looked down onto the floor and nodded my head. "Holy shit, Presley. You never cease to amaze me girl."

"I'm such a slut. And Eve has that video and she's gonna show everyone. My aunt will kill me for ruining her reputation." I cried. Jameson wrapped his arms around me and I cried harder.

"Now you know that's not true. And I know that you wouldn't be so upset if Killian and Xavier, both, meant something to you."

"They do. I think I'm falling in love with them both. And that's what they want, what I want and it's all been ruined."

"Own it. It can only destroy you if you let it. No one is going to listen to Eve's crazy rambling." Jameson rubbed my back and kissed the top of my head. I was an only child but if I were to have a brother, my relationship with Jameson was exactly how I imagined it to feel.

"Presley?" I jumped at the sound of Killian's voice and looked towards him standing in the doorway of the galley. Arms folded and dressed all in black. He tried to mask the look of concern on his face, just like I had to stop myself from throwing myself into his arms for comfort. I didn't dare in case Eve walked into the room and everything got ten times worse.

"Eve." Jameson explained. "Sir, I don't mean to overstep by talking about this." Jameson unwrapped me from his body and stepped forward. "She has a video. A video of you, Captain Xavier and Presley. Now she's threatening to show it to the crew, our community, just to ruin Presley." Killian had blood-boiling anger all over his face. "We all know that Eve is infatuated with Xavier and her obsession has gone too far."

"What video?" Killian asked. I looked away from him.

"Last night, when we were all together in the cabin." I answered. "She's given me six hours to leave."

"No! She's fired and she will be the one, out of here in six hours." I never thought I would see Killian so angry.

"Like I have a choice!" I shouted, my emotions getting the best of me. "She'll show everyone that video." I wiped my eyes with the back of my hand. Killian stepped forward and cupped my face.

"No, she won't. I told you that your job is safe, and that means I will do anything to protect your reputation."

"I'm scared. Why am I being punished for falling in love?" I whispered. Killian smiled and planted a sweet and gentle kiss on my lips, despite Jameson being beside us.

"You're not. Falling in love is nothing to be punished for." He whispered against my lips. "We won't let anyone hurt you, you are ours."

chapter eighteen

I WAS CHEWING ON my lips in anticipation. I had curled myself up on the sofa in the bridge. Xavier and Killian talking among themselves. I was watching the clock, five hours to go, and Eve would make sure my entire life was falling to pieces, just because she was jealous.

I glanced at Xavier, he brushed a hand through his hair as he looked over Eve's contract. The sun was shining through the windows and framed him just perfectly, Captain of the Sea. His brows were furrowed as he read. I smiled to myself, I was truly falling in love. I looked at Killian, sitting in the Captain's chair. I was falling in love with them both.

"We can pay her until the end of the season, she leaves today." Xavier shrugged and passed the papers to Killian. He flicked over them and chucked them on the console.

"She's lucky I'm willing to do that." Killian snarled.

"What about the video?" I asked. Both of the men, my men, looked at me. Killian stood and came to sit next to me, pulling me into his side, arm around my shoulders. He kissed the top of my head.

"We'll get rid of it, and if she refuses then we'll call the police. No one is going to see it, I'll sue her ass before they can." I chuckled at his billionaire talk, Xavier joined us, reaching out for my hand and intertwining our fingers.

"We're together, Pres. We're adults and what we decide to do with our lives is up to us." Xavier spoke.

"Eve will be gone. And they'll be a nice spot open for Chief Stew." Killian nudged me.

"I don't want that." I looked at him. "You know that's not the dream, and there's someone that deserves that role much more than me," I explained. "Chessa works her ass off everyday, even if they're friends, she's had to put up with Eve a lot longer than me."

"Let's go sort this out." Xavier said.

The three of us left the bridge, Xavier and Killian taking the lead. Eve was in the main salon, sitting at the interior laptop with her earphones in. I quickly scurried off as they grabbed her attention. I walked into the galley, which was empty and down into the crew mess.

The rest of the crew were sitting around the crew table eating breakfast, and as soon as I took that last step I could hear the commotion beginning upstairs. Which grabbed everyone's attention, their eyes landing on me.

"Hey girl, want some of James's breakfast tots?" May called.

"What's going on up there?" Ben asked with a mouthful of James potatoes with bacon bits.

"I-umm." My stumbling got me caught red-handed, but I couldn't say anything before Eve came storming down the stairs and shoving me out of the way. She grabbed me by the shoulders and pushed me against the wall. The loud thuds of Killian and Xavier coming down the stairs followed.

"You whore." Eve snarled at me.

"Get the fuck off me." I tried to push her off.

"Leave her alone." Xavier managed to pull her away as she scraped to get at me again.

"What's going on?" Phoenix asked, standing up.

"Perfect Presley is fucking Xavier. She's fucking Killian too. Both of them like the whore she is." Eve screamed.

You could cut the atmosphere with a knife. It was filled with a heavy silence. I closed my eyes but that didn't stop the world from spinning.

"Eve, your employment is terminated and you need to leave the boat immediately." I heard Killian.

"This is unbelievable." Eve snarled.

"Pres." May stood in front of me and shook me gently. "Let's take you to get some fresh air." I opened my eyes and latched onto her hand, ignoring everyone else in the room as she pulled me up the stairs.

May led me off the boat and we sat down at the edge of the dock, being off the boat gave me a breath of fresh air. I sat watching the water knock off the side of the dock, the sound helped settle my breathing.

"So what Eve said…" May's voice trailed off. I took a glance at her, then nodded.

"I didn't expect it to happen, didn't know if it could happen. Falling for two men and them being completely fine with that. And last night we went to dinner and we talked about the fact I had feelings for them both. We slept together after we all came back. Eve recorded us and I guess the door wasn't closed properly, or maybe she opened it, I don't know." I shook my head.

"Wow."

"Yeah, wow. I think the worst part is that last night, I was happy and something so good has been stained."

"I'm sorry, Pres." She put her hand on top of mine.

"I never thought this would happen. It's not what I wanted to happen."

"Eve's been fired, and trust me no one else is going to care. We're a family."

"The cardinal rule is not to shit where you eat, and the captain and the owner? Everyone is going to have a field day."

"And so what? Phoenix and I do it in the lazarette almost daily." I blinked.

"You and Phoenix?" I repeated and she smirked.

"He is very good with his mouth." She wriggled her brows, and I laughed.

The carefree moment was ruined by the sound of suitcase wheels running down the gangway. Killian and Xavier follow her. Eve dragged her case onto the deck and looked at me. May got up and stood in front of me. Killian and Xavier blocked her too and Eve strutted off down the dock.

My two men walked over to us.

"We'll take it from here, thanks May."

"Yeah, of course. I'll see you later, girlie." May smiled down at me and walked back onto the boat.

Xavier held out his hand, I took his hand and he pulled me up.

"She's gone." He told me.

"And I have this." Killian pulled a phone out of his pocket. "The video won't see daylight." He tossed the phone into a gap of water and I watched it sink to the bottom. A weight lifted from my shoulders. Killian wrapped his arms around me from behind. And Xavier from the front. I was enclosed between the two of them and I felt the safest I had ever been in my life.

"I love you," I whispered. "Both of you."

"I love you too." Xavier leant down to kiss me.

"I love you, my love." Killian whispered in my ear as I kissed Xavier back. Once Xavier had pulled away, Killian tipped my head back towards him so he could have his turn.

"Come on work to do." Xavier chuckled. "We will finish this later."

"Round two?" I smirked, as I was released.

"And round three." Killian smacked my ass and I giggled as we walked back onto the boat, together.

acknowledgements

Thank you to everyone who has read my books, and I hope you love this hardback edition. First of all, a big shout out to my author besties, Emma and Faith, for their support in the past year, I would not have reached this point without you and probably retreated back into my cave.

Al, I say this all the time but thank you for being my best friend through thick and thin. You've been around since I first started publishing and one of my greatest cheerleaders since day one. Not only that but thanks to you I met T.

T Cake, my hype woman, I will never forget you sitting on my sofa with your highlighter proof reading for me. I'm so lucky to have you in my life.

about the author

Em Solstice is a romance author from the UK. As well as procrastinating writing fast-paced novellas with a spicy twist, she enjoys snuggling her cat and drinking Starbucks... and waiting for her own love story to begin.